Zach murmured, "a problem."

Bett shook her head drowsily. "*You* may have a problem. *I* have no problems of any kind." She curled her arms around his waist, snuggling closer to his bare, warm flesh. It seemed like a wonderful idea to stay just as they were. At least for the next hundred hours.

"You can be a disgracefully wanton woman, two bits." He nuzzled at the delectable hollow in her shoulder.

"Thank you."

"Insatiable."

"Yes."

"Uninhibited."

She opened one sleepy eye. "Where are all these compliments leading?"

Jeanne Grant *is a native of Michigan, where she and her husband own cherry and peach orchards, and also grow strawberries. In addition to raising two children, she has worked as a teacher, counselor, and personnel manager. Jeanne began writing at age ten. She's an avid reader as well, and says, "I don't think anything will ever beat a good love story."*

Dear Reader:

One year ago, at a time when romance readers were asking for "something different," we took a bold step in romance publishing by launching an innovative new series of books about married love: TO HAVE AND TO HOLD.

Since then, TO HAVE AND TO HOLD has developed a faithful following of enthusiastic readers. We're still delighted to receive your letters—which come from teenagers, grandmothers, and women of every age in between, both married and single. All of you have one quality in common—you believe that love and romance exist beyond the "happily ever after" endings of more conventional stories.

In the months to come, we will continue to offer romance reading of the highest caliber in TO HAVE AND TO HOLD. Next month, keep an eye out for another book by our very popular Jeanne Grant—*Conquer the Memories*. Jennifer Rose also returns in December with *Pennies From Heaven*, and Kate Nevins, whom some of you know as the author of several SECOND CHANCE AT LOVE romances, has written her first TO HAVE AND TO HOLD, *Memory and Desire,* coming in January. Be sure, too, not to overlook the "newcomers" you'll continue to see in TO HAVE AND TO HOLD. In December, Joan Darling debuts with *Tyler's Folly,* a unique, witty story that made me laugh out loud. We're proud to bring these wonderfully talented writers to you.

Warmest wishes,

Ellen Edwards

Ellen Edwards, Senior Editor
TO HAVE AND TO HOLD
The Berkley Publishing Group
200 Madison Avenue
New York, N.Y. 10016

CUPID'S
CONFEDERATES

JEANNE
GRANT

**SECOND CHANCE AT LOVE
BOOK**

Other books by *Jeanne Grant*

Second Chance at Love
MAN FROM TENNESSEE   #49
A DARING PROPOSITION   #149
KISSES FROM HEAVEN   #167
WINTERGREEN   #184
SILVER AND SPICE   #220

To Have and to Hold
SUNBURST   #14
TROUBLE IN PARADISE   #28

To All My Moms

None of whom remotely resemble Elizabeth

1

REACHING UNDER THE netting, Bett brushed a trickle of perspiration from her forehead, bent back over the bee-hive, and started singing again in a low, husky murmur. *"Doucement, ce n'est que moi. Doucement, mes amants charmants, doucement..."*

The temperature on this August day was 95; Bett was sweltering in ragged jeans, halter top, and shoulder-length netting, and frankly wasn't in the mood to croon seductive sweet nothings to anyone. Still, one didn't quarrel with success. This particular clan of honeybees was touchy. And if they wanted French love words set in song, the little darlings got them.

A dusty cloud of wings buzzed up in protest as she uncovered the "super"—the top shelf in the man-made hive. The honey in the super was surplus, and removing it wouldn't harm the hive in any way. In a few more weeks, Bett would have to convince the bees of that; at the moment, she was simply checking on their production and health. Unfortunately, the worker bees were quite annoyed with her. Bett felt sympathy; they had undoubt-edly spent the entire day frantically fanning their queen to keep her cool, and now Bett had destroyed all their

1

air conditioning. But as the smell of warm honey wafted through the sultry air, she frowned. A dozen bees settled on her gently moving bare hand; she paid no attention as she bent lower. Below the super was the largest part of the hive, where the bees stored their own food as well as brood combs for the young.

It was loaded. The hive would swarm and divide into two separate hives if one became overcrowded; to avoid that Bett would have to isolate the bees, and soon.

The thought of handling a swarm didn't bother her; she'd done it before. But the last time, the swarming hive had settled in the top of a plum tree, and Zach had lain there on the ground rolling with laughter as he watched her climb after them, only to have them shift to the top of another tree. For an entire afternoon, the swarm and Bett had played leapfrog between treetops. She'd tickled her husband unmercifully when it was over.

There were a great many occasions in Bett's five-year-old marriage when her husband's wayward sense of humor required a strong hand.

Reclosing the hive, Bett stood up and gently brushed the last cluster of bees from her shoulders and arms. They fluttered back to their business and Bett stretched, kneading her small fists in the hollow of her back. Her mind was busy cataloguing the rest of the day's responsibilities. At least the morning's peach picking was done, and Zach would handle the semi coming in that night; but someone still had to go for more bushel baskets, look at the garden, oil and fuel the Massey for tomorrow . . . Then, too, Zach seemed to have this strange idea that the bills on the desk should at least be opened . . . the list kept rolling. By the time she came to the zillionth chore, another trickle of perspiration was sliding between her eyes, and she came to the logical conclusion that it was past time for a ten-minute break.

With a springy step, Bett wandered out of the plum orchard and up a knoll blanketed ꞏ ith clover and wild flowers. Whipping off her veiled straw hat—a makeshift beekeeper's garb at best—she felt her baby-fine blond hair shiver down to her shoulders, the same baby-fine hair that had been ruthlessly confined to a rubber band that morning. Confined for about three minutes, anyway. Not that Bett hadn't tried all ninety-nine hair products guaranteed to thicken and manage, but beyond hating the women in the hair-care commercials, she'd given up finding a cure for too-soft, too-fine hair. Now, she just let it have its way and tried to keep the style simple.

Another bead of moisture trickled down between her breasts and blended with a little peach fuzz left over from the morning's picking. It itched. Actually, just about her whole body itched. Her jeans were sticking to her like miracle glue; the terry-cloth halter top was as absorbent as a towel; and if another soul were anywhere near her, she would be having an anxiety attack about deodorant fadeout.

But then, there wasn't another soul around. Just past the rise of the clover field were the woods, nine luscious acres of ironwood and hickory and walnut—the same nine acres that could have been sold as timber to pay off their monstrous operating loan except that both Bett and Zach would sell their souls first. The woods held solace and silence; how could anyone sell that? In the spring, the ground there was carpeted with violets and trillium; in the fall, wild animals built shelters in the depths of leaves and hollows.

And on a blistering day like this one, Bett felt instant relief in the cool shadows. She paused, her bright eyes surveying the splendid view. Their pond stretched out in a long lazy S, its spring-fed waters glittering in the sun. Wild flowers crept up to the shore, mingling with cattails. Beyond the pond stretched a twenty-acre slope of peach trees. She could see the glint of coral even from here, and the sweet smell of ripening fruit drifted toward her. Her dad would have loved the farm so much, Bett thought idly, and unconsciously bit her lip in remembered loss.

The town of Silver Oaks was a fifteen-minute drive from Lake Michigan. The lake was a little less than a lady, Zach often said. A storm would start in Washington, build up power in Idaho, gain fury in Montana and the Dakotas, be a raging tempest by the time it reached Wisconsin—and immediately settle down for Her Highness, the Lake. Michigan's western coast suffered only the gentler breezes, and the promise of regular, nurturing rains and temperate winters. This was orchard land, a sandy loam with a mild roll and contour to the landscape.

Bett and Zach had first seen the area in springtime. Zach's Uncle John had willed him the farm, for no known reason since Zach had only met the man once. Neither Zach nor Bett had the least idea what to do with his inheritance, particularly once they understood that three-quarters of the 250 acres of orchard land had been given over to grain. This was due not to mismanagement but to Uncle John's age and failing health. Grain was easier to take care of. In the meantime, though, it would have taken a fortune to turn the property back to the profitable orchard ground it was meant to be. A fortune Bett and Zach didn't have. So, obviously, their only choice was to sell it.

But in the spring that whole countryside turned into a fairyland. Acre on acre burst into blossom until one saw pink and white for miles. The perfume was inescapable; it seeped through closed doors and shuttered windows, inside, outside, everywhere. From a distance, an orchard of peaches in bloom had the look of acres of fragile cotton candy. Close up, the petals fluttered down with only a whisper of wind; the earth looked frosted with pink and white, and if one happened to find oneself making love in such an orchard on a spring day for no reason at all, well...It had been damn tough for Bett to go back to teaching high school French in Milwaukee.

In June, they returned, this time for good. Everyone

said they were crazy to come here. Everyone was absolutely right. They knew nothing about farming. Bett was twenty-one, with a B.A. in French; Zach was twenty-three and had just completed his second year of law school; they were both very happy, that first year of their marriage . . . and one look at the land had caught both of them, like rabbits in a snare. There'd been no going back.

Bett's wandering eye paused again, this time catching sight of something strangely out of sync in the natural landscape. *Definitely* out of sync. A very old boot was weaving back and forth in the air, the ankle to which it was attached resting on a jean-clad knee. The owner of the boot was lying flat in the grass by the pond, his shortsleeved shirt open and his head resting on a log. His eyes were closed and a long blade of grass was stuck between his teeth.

So. Guess who else had had the unforgivable idea of taking a break when they had work absolutely coming out of their ears. Bett tossed her hat on the ground; her halter top followed rapidly. The sneaky piece of manhood down there certainly looked as though he'd just emerged from a haystack, not at all like a once-very-serious law student. Well, he might still look halfway intelligent. *If* he took the blade of grass out of his mouth.

She tugged open the button on her jeans, then used the toe of one boot to pry off the heel of the other. That lazy Tom Sawyer was just lying there without a care in the world, while his virtuous wife had been *slaving* the entire morning. Even reclining, he looked tall and lanky. Big feet. Lustrous, thick brown hair, coppery skin, and a square face with clean, precise lines. Blue eyes—but not at all like her own blue eyes. Hers were plain old blue; his were Spencer Tracy sassy, the kind of eyes that took their humor slow and lazy. He wasn't very smart—no one with any intelligence worked his way through college with all A's, completed two years of law school, and then fell for a derelict old mismanaged farm—but

Bett was rather attached to him. For one thing, he generally handled the impulsive surprises she handed out pretty well.

With an impish grin, she left her jeans in a heap—her underpants had naturally come off with them—and tiptoed out into the sun.

Zach lifted one lazy eyebrow at the sound of the splash, then the second one when he glimpsed the distinct flash of a bare white thigh. He hunkered up just a little higher on the fallen log to get a better view, carefully making sure his eyes were closed every time the mermaid surfaced for air—and to look his way.

Sleek white limbs skimmed gracefully just beneath the water's surface; a stream of long blond hair swirled around her shoulders. Bett was built like a miniature, compact, exquisitely detailed time bomb. How in the hell had he ever married such a tease?

He stretched out one leg to better view Bett's back float. It was only for a minute; Bett was a terrific swimmer, but a lousy floater. She sank. Not before she'd shown off exactly what she'd intended to. Two tiny, wrinkled nipples that looked in terrible danger of being sunburned; they were that vulnerable.

Cautiously, he pushed off one boot, then the other. Every farmer in the area joked that all libido simply died in the summer; somehow, Zach seemed to have the opposite problem. Maybe it had to do with knowing that he and Bett shared the same workday, struggled through the endless hours together, and still loved what they were doing. Who could have guessed that Bett would fall for the land the way he had?

She was built on such tiny, fragile lines. A long white throat and those huge, lustrous blue eyes, the cloud of blond hair . . . she would outwork him, if he let her. He didn't. A man had to put his foot down now and then, just in case male chauvinism came back in style.

Evidently she was weary of playing porpoise, because she suddenly faced his half-closed eyes with a disgusted expression. Slowly, she swam closer to shore. Zach never once flickered an eyelid to let on he was awake, but he could see her through lowered lashes. Her shoulders emerged first from the water, golden and smooth. Then her breasts, small and taut, water streaming down the crevice between. She'd promised him she would develop a bustier figure once they married and she gained a little weight.

They'd married. She'd never gained any weight. Her waist was still nipped in, her hips almost nonexistent. Just now, her hair was a single rope-strand hanging over one shoulder, dripping a long trail of water between her breasts and over a flat, satiny tummy into a soft curl of golden hair. She had golden skin, like their sun-kissed peaches. A soft, smooth gold.

She really didn't have a damn thing to flaunt in the way of a figure. She was flaunting it, both hands on her slim hips, head proudly thrown back. The sun caught her delicate profile, every bone, every hollow and shadow. His jeans could barely accommodate the growth within. If he were any closer to her, she wouldn't still be standing.

Bett was a witch. He'd actually married a witch. In college, he'd specialized in voluptuous Amazons. He still didn't know what had happened. From the back, Bett could pass for a boy. And from the front... Bett could be sensitive about her lack of build. Foolishly sensitive. Every miniature inch of her aroused lust in him.

"*Hi.*"

Even her voice did it. A husky little alto. She was so darned slight that her surprisingly sexy voice always drove him slightly over the edge. Zach managed to very slowly open his eyes, feigning surprise. "Bett?"

"Hmm?"

"You're in trouble."

He didn't even bother to look, taking the three steps to the water with his arms extended for a racing dive. He knew every inch of the pond and he knew its depth at that point, and he could care less if his clothes got wet. In seconds, the shockingly cool water closed over his head.

Laughing, Bett pulled herself out on the other side of the pond and started running, grabbing her jeans and halter top and hat and boots as she ran.

"You come back here!" shouted a baritone voice behind her, but she paid no attention.

They both had work to do, she told herself virtuously. Not necessarily work that she'd planned to do naked, but then the picking crew had been sent home at noon, which left their 250 acres empty of voyeurs. Their neighbor Grady was an obvious risk, but since he was Grady, and of an age, Bett didn't give him more than a passing thought. The rough clover field chafed her bare feet, but she kept up her pace. Knowing Zach . . .

Through the clover, past the plum trees, past her hives; there the truck was waiting. She vaulted into the cab, slid her cool, damp bottom onto the aged vinyl, tossed her clothes on the seat, and started the engine as she faced a languid Sniper. She told the cat for the thousandth time that no self-respecting feline liked to ride in vehicles. Sniper stretched every Persian inch of him and started purring as the engine coughed and sputtered to life. The Ford pickup was ancient, but for another year or two they couldn't afford a new one.

And Bett couldn't afford a new husband. Besides, she liked the one she had. Zach was made on confident, easygoing lines; it did him good to get shaken up once in a while. The mischievous grin persisted all through the drive to the house, during the hurried rush into a clean pair of jeans and a T-shirt, on the trip to the local market to pick up a load of bushel baskets, and through another trip to a processor to request the return of their pallets by morning.

Three hours later, she was unloading the bushel baskets with a forklift when Grady drove in, his dusty red pickup unmistakable. Bett leaped down from the forklift just as their neighbor approached her, the last of the afternoon's hot sun behind him.

Grady Caldwell's face had a permanently hangdog look, with pendulous jowls and lots of wrinkles. He was hitching up his trousers as he approached, already taking his pipe out of his pocket to pack it. She'd never seen him light the pipe, but it did take a lot of packing. Grady claimed to be sixty; Bett was fairly certain that his sixtieth birthday had passed a decade ago, and regularly marveled at the relationship between men and vanity.

"Where's your better half?" he asked gruffly.

"Are you kidding? You've got it," Bett replied impishly. "Are you coming in for iced tea?"

"Haven't time." Grady pushed back his cap and with it a strand of perspiration beads on his forehead. "Still damn hot." Grady never risked any extra words.

"Yes," Bett agreed.

"Been through those young peaches you kids planted in the spring," he grumbled, and packed his pipe. And packed his pipe.

"We've been worried about how they'd do with this heat." Bett resisted the urge to gnaw her fingernails, waiting for her neighbor's judgment. Was there something wrong, some bug in the peaches they hadn't known to look for? But she knew better than to hurry Grady. When they'd moved here, Grady was the first to hustle over and tell them that nobody with the brain of a flea would take on a business without knowing a blessed thing about it . . . but then, Grady was the one who helped turn that around. Without his advice and lectures, they probably would have gotten nowhere. Bett could still remember how the three of them walked every inch of the land

and even tasted the dirt from spot to spot—an experience she valued, and never intended to repeat.

"Looks fine," Grady said finally, totally bored. "Must be a good moisture base in the soil, just like Zach said. Taken on growth even this last week in the heat. Probably make a fortune on the damn things."

Bett relaxed. "It was nice of you to take the time, Grady. I have to admit that for the entire last month both of us have barely set foot in the orchard."

"'Course you haven't. You two are too busy taking on too much; wouldn't kill you to hire a little extra help, you know. Useless talking to you," Grady said disgustedly.

Bett interpreted that as high praise. Working oneself to death rated respect from Grady. "We're doing okay."

"You don't know where I could catch up with Zach?"

From the cloud of dust coming from the hill beyond the barn, she could make a shrewd guess. "Could I help you in the meantime?" she asked.

"Got a tractor needs an O-ring, and Brown's is out."

"Out of my bailiwick," Bett admitted.

Grady gave her a sidelong glance. "I've seen lots worse with a tractor than you."

Bett stuffed her hands in her back pockets. The cloud of dust came closer; Zach was driving the old 350 tractor. She didn't try to continue the conversation with Grady. At first she'd been offended by his brusque attitude, until she'd caught on. Grady was basically terrified of women. Such casual compliments as the one he'd just handed her made him turn beet red. Lobsterish at the moment. And one of these days she was going to give him a big hug and probably scare the pipe right out of his hand.

Zach sprang down from the tractor with a welcoming smile for his neighbor. He did not, Bett noticed, even glance her way. As he strode forward, she couldn't help but notice that his shirt had dried in a disastrously wrinkled fashion since his dunking some three hours before.

She was about to inquire innocently about his disgraceful appearance when she felt a solid slap on her backside, followed by the welcome weight of his arm around her shoulders. She returned the hug. Grady, as usual, ignored any hint of a personal exchange between them.

"What's up?" Zach asked him.

"O-rings. Damn Brown can't get his till tomorrow, and I got a field needs spraying tonight. And the only tractor I got free—"

"Your John Deere or the Massey?" Zach questioned.

"The John Deere." Grady paused, jutting a wiry leg forward. "And I wanted to tell you those young peaches look good. You keep a fresh mow like I told you. Don't want weeds leaching any moisture in this weather."

Bett only half listened to the farmer talk, more interested in the feel of Zach's arm on her shoulders, the graze of his shirt against hers. Her husband radiated warmth, strength, and the exhaustion of a man who took too few ten-minute breaks—plus a purely virile message that raised her blood pressure. He still hadn't looked her in the eye.

"Can you give me some idea of what time you want dinner, Zach?" she interrupted them finally.

"I'll be in as soon as we've fixed up Grady's tractor. *Bett.*"

She was about to make for the house when he hooked an arm around her waist and turned her. He was definitely looking her in the eye this time, from about four inches away. Those eyes of his were promising endless retribution for her mischief at the pond.

"You go in, take a shower, and relax with an iced tea," he ordered. "You were up before I was this morning. I'll worry about dinner."

"Sure," Bett agreed, and added demurely, "sir." She did like a dominating man. And in the meantime, knowing that Grady had a penchant for long-winded conversations, she figured she could at least get the bills opened and the house in livable order before Zach came in.

"I mean it," Zach said roughly.

She kissed him on the cheek. Grady packed his pipe a mile a minute. After a moment, the two men strode off toward the shop in the barn. Bett stood for just a minute longer in the yard, surrounded by fading sunlight and the dust of an impossibly hot day.

The huge old barn cast gray shadows on the yellow farmyard. Every muscle in her body ached from weariness, yet Bett's mind was on the semi due in after dinner to load up their peaches from the morning's pick. Only Zach looked tired. Overtired.

Scolding him would do no good at all. Seducing him directly after dinner might—yes, a nice, totally degenerate, wanton, explosive interlude of lovemaking should do the trick. She could guarantee that Zach would fall asleep afterward. Then she could load the truck by herself and finish up the rest of the next day's work preparations. He'd never even know.

The plan was excellent. Bett nodded approvingly and headed for the house. She was hotter than an iron, her feet were killing her, and the nape of her neck was prickly under the weight of her shoulder-length hair. But handling her difficult-to-manage husband took priority over her own physical discomforts.

They took care of each other. They had that kind of marriage. Zach was her strength, her laughter, her entire definition of love. There were times when it took every ounce of imagination she had to subtly keep him in his place. Next to her.

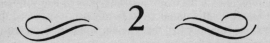

2

BETT SLIPPED OUT of her work boots and her socks at the door, wiggled her toes, and padded barefoot on the cool terra-cotta floor toward the kitchen. Ignoring a disgraceful layer of dust and casual clutter, her eyes swept over the rest of the downstairs en route, loving it. Their underground house was in the shape of a half-moon, and except for the structural dome and the glass, she and Zach had built it all themselves last winter.

The main floor sprawled around a central double-opening fieldstone fireplace. Sunlight poured into both the living room and kitchen from their shared southern exposure; hidden in the rear of the house were the pantry, the bath, the laundry, and Zach's study. Gently curving walls on the main floor climbed to a vaulted ceiling above, where huge semicircular windows encouraged sunlight to pour into the bedrooms. An open stairway led upward.

There was a mood of space and openness to the entire house. Plants in carved crockery brought the outside in; two leaf-green couches formed a conversation cluster; an old deacon's bench leaned against the curved wall of the living room. The bookcases were generous; Zach and Bett were both insatiable readers, at least in the winter.

Generally, there was a splash of fresh flowers somewhere.

The place wasn't overcrowded with furniture. Neither
wanted to burden their space with excess furnishings,
even if they'd had the money to do so. Truthfully, the
last thing they'd needed was the expense of a new house,
but Uncle John's derelict old farmhouse had forced the
decision. Not only had that ancient structure been crum-
bling from the foundations, but the furnace worked only
from June until August; lights gratuitously went on in
the middle of the night; and the plumbing only made a
tired effort. It would have taken more money to fix up
Uncle John's house than to build their own. This one,
at least, hadn't been outrageously costly, both because
they'd done most of the work themselves and because
Zach was a maniac about energy conservation.

And to Bett, their place was distinctly *theirs*. In summer, they could collapse into a chair in filthy jeans,
drinking iced tea while waiting for the next crisis. In
winter, they could dress up on a special evening and sip
honey wine in front of the fire and feel very, very luxurious. The house just fit them. And where else could a
married couple say they'd made love on a gently sloping,
grass-cushioned roof?

You're digressing again, Bett told herself, and opened
the refrigerator. Stop thinking about sex. Think
about . . . money. Or babies.

Nothing in the refrigerator announced itself as irresistible. She closed the door and ambled back to the desk
in Zach's study to attack the bills. Slitting the first en-
velope, she noted that the local fuel deliverer had put a
sticker of a smiling face on the invoice, which indicated
that they owed him a whopping $939. George had such
a sense of humor. She hoped his humor would last until
they were paid for last Monday's peaches.

Babies were more fun to think about than money,

anyway. Actually, the diapered species was another of their motivations for building a house. Upstairs there happened to be three spacious rooms—one the master bedroom, one a combination spare room and storage niche that Bett promised herself regularly she would organize, and the third . . . the third room was still unpainted, still empty. Waiting. This was the room she and Zach had designated as the nursery.

This year they hoped to finish paying off their major loan from the bank, and next year they had additional orchards finally coming into production. Babies were just about ready to be slotted into the agenda. They'd been practicing to make them for some time. Zach, probably because he had been orphaned as a teenager, wanted a hundred. Bett would have settled for one. At times, the nesting urge would fill her with longing, but then Zach would really get in the spirit of practicing again . . .

You have a one-track mind this evening, she scolded herself and went upstairs. After taking a quick shower, she donned a pair of old white jeans and a T-shirt of Zach's, then padded barefoot down to the kitchen again. After swiping the counter with a sponge and popping the lunch dishes into the dishwasher, she reopened the refrigerator, hoping that this time a decision about dinner would miraculously occur to her.

It didn't. The only thought that did occur to her was that her mother would disown her for the way she kept house and organized meals. The thought of her mom instantly sent a wave of uneasiness through Bett's mind. Elizabeth was in Milwaukee, only a few hours' drive by car. When Bett was being honest with herself, she considered that distance exactly enough; she was able to see Elizabeth often without the two women being on top of each other. Not that they didn't care about and love each other, but having such very different values, they inevitably, and sometimes sadly, clashed.

Bett stared at the offerings in the refrigerator, unconsciously biting her lip. Her father had died exactly thirteen months and four days ago; she was not likely to forget. She and her dad had been a matched pair; they both liked football games on Sunday afternoons and fooling around in the yard and talking with their feet propped up on the coffee table. Her mother was not at all that way. Elizabeth had not been coping well since Chet's death. Bett was at a loss, not knowing how to help her mother, who was so different from her in every way. That geographical distance had begun to seem something she should feel guilty about.

"Bett?"

She chuckled at Zach's growl, other thoughts chased away. Her husband was hardly likely to forget her desertion at the pond. Zack strode into the kitchen and paused, hands on hips, watching her as she started to prepare a picnic dinner of ham slices, cheese, fresh fruit, and raw vegetables with dip. It was too hot for heavier fare, anyway.

"Did I or did I not tell you to come in here and put your feet up?" he asked mildly.

"Oh, Lord. I haven't disobeyed another order?"

"You have." Zach took a tray from above the refrigerator and nudged her aside with his hip to finish what she'd started. "You were in enough disgrace already," he mentioned over his shoulder.

"Oh?" The sun had turned his skin bronze over the summer, a bronze that delightfully set off his light eyes. She'd always basically disliked the muscle-bound type, but she was extremely fond of Zach's muscles, primarily because his sinew was attached to a lean frame that radiated sheer maleness whenever he moved. Fluid was the word. His body was tough and hard; inside, though she'd never tell him, there was tender stuff. Gentleness, even, when no one was looking and the lights were off. "So your swim felt good?" she asked idly. "Lord, it was hot this afternoon. Did you get Grady's tractor fixed?"

"The tractor's fixed, the semi's already been here to pick up the peaches, the equipment's all ready for tomorrow . . . and *anyone* could have been driving around the farm while you were streaking about naked."

She followed Zach into the living room, carrying the smaller tray with iced-tea glasses and silverware. "I wasn't *streaking* about naked. I took a quick dip in the pond to cool off. The bees have to be separated or they're going to swarm," she added seriously.

"How's the honey production?"

They settled themselves on facing couches. "Absolutely stupendous. Mead time this fall."

"Oh, Lord." His wry grin made her chuckle. There was nothing messier than making mead, or honey wine. It took them a full fall afternoon of sticky sweet messes that had become a tradition . . . as was the one evening a year when they both became perfectly silly on the stuff, once it was finished fermenting.

Zach didn't waste any time dipping into the platter of fresh food. "You were *not* just taking a quick dip in the pond to cool off. You were flaunting again."

"I never did understand why I married a man with such a dirty mind. I was simply swimming," Bett said virtuously, and dove into her own plate.

"Bull. You knew I'd come after you."

She leveled him a scolding frown, between grabbing a slice of cucumber and smothering it with dip. "You've accused me of this kind of thing before, you know. And I've explained to you that my mother raised a shy, modest type, hardly an exhibitionist . . . Did you check the peaches for tomorrow?"

"The north fifteen. We'll probably spot-pick in the orchard behind the house as well. They're nearly ready, and with this heat they could turn by tomorrow. Did you get the baskets?"

"At a discount."

"How'd you manage that?" Zach shoved a foot against the coffee table.

"Seduced Kramer."

"That must have taken dedication."

"It did," Bett said fervently.

"Dedication, courage, and a cast-iron stomach."

"Well, you know me," Bett agreed. "I was desperate. Couldn't get anyone's attention down by the pond..."

"For two cents, Mrs. Monroe, I'd probably beat you."

By some coincidence, Bett found three pennies in her jeans pocket. She tossed him two, and waited interestedly.

Zach got up, all right, but only to answer the second ring of the telephone. The phone inevitably rang off the hook in the early evening. Farmers calling farmers, primarily to encourage each other's heart attacks. The forecast was for the heat wave to continue tomorrow, and once the weather report was over the anxiety attacks began.

Bett leaned back against the couch, half closed her eyes, and felt gentle waves of weariness invade every limb. At least they didn't have to go back out again tonight, since the semi had already been in. Not that their garden wasn't begging for an hour of attention, but her priority was a little intimate time with Zach. December was full of leisure time, but minutes had to count in August.

"It's your mother."

Zach watched his wife's face instantly change from serene, satisfied weariness to taut stress as she lurched up to reach for the phone.

"Mom? How are you?" Unconsciously, Bett pushed back her cloud of yellow hair, jerked off the couch like the coil of a spring, and started winding and rewinding the phone cord around her finger.

Zach began piling empty plates on the tray, resisting the urge to clatter them together. Bett had always called her mother at least weekly; lately, Elizabeth had taken to calling every other day. Zach was fond of his mother-in-law and certainly felt sympathy for her trouble adjusting since Chet's death. But that sympathy had been gradually eroding away for months. Bett was torn apart every time the phone rang.

"Stop crying." Bett's gentle voice was laced with anxiety. "Mom, you can't keep doing this. It's been well over a year. Did you get involved with that women's club you said you were going to join?"

Silently, Zach carted the trays to the kitchen. By the time he'd taken care of the few dishes, Bett had the phone cord wrapped around her waist and one slim hand was raking through her hair. She was facing away from him as he stood in the doorway. Her spine was as taut as a violin string, and when she half turned again her eyes were tightly closed.

"Mom, I *know* the house has memories for you. Have you even asked Martha if she wanted to move in with you? Since her husband died, she's had the same problem sleeping nights, hasn't she?" Bett twisted the cord around and around her finger until her finger turned white from lack of circulation, then uncoiled it impatiently. "No, of *course* I'm not saying you should sell the house if you don't want to. It's just that if staying there is still making you unhappy after all this time..."

Zach set a glass of sun tea on the coffee table for Bett, and carried his own over to the fieldstone fireplace. He leaned back against the rough stone, staring outside at the last of the sunset.

Bett rubbed her temple with two fingers, denting the soft flesh and making white marks. *"Mom.* Please, please, just tell me what you want me to do! Anything, darling. Do you want me to come for a couple of days? Do you want me to pack the things up and sell the house for you? I'll do whatever you want; you must know that. You just have to tell me *what* you want. Mom, this *has* to stop—" Bett could feel her eyes filling up with ridiculous, overemotional tears.

Zach's tea glass clattered down on the mantel. In four long strides, he reached her, untangled enough of the phone cord to claim the phone, and all but jammed the receiver against his ear.

"Liz? This is Zach. Your daughter's in trouble." The words, however impromptu, were calculated to bring an instant cessation of feminine tears at the other end. They worked. Bett was staring up at him blankly, her lips parted in shock. He unwrapped the phone cord from around her and, with a brusque motion of his hand, urged her to sit on the couch. He kept on talking. "What would you say to coming to stay with us for a while? Bett's got so much to do she's running herself down... Yes, I know, but then she wouldn't ask for help if she were sitting in the middle of a flood; we both know that... I don't know. Does it matter? Why don't you just pack a suitcase and close up the house, and we'll worry about the how-long of it another time. *No,* Liz. We are *not* thinking about selling the farm and going sane again."

He had to listen to something or other about the care of her dahlias before she agreed to come. Used to Elizabeth, he paid no attention. But when he hung up the phone, Bett was standing in the middle of the room with her arms wrapped around her chest. Her small spray of tears had dried. Zach sighed, calmly walking over to her and brushing back her silky hair with gentle fingers. "You've wanted your mother here for a long time now, haven't you? But you were afraid to say anything. We've both gotten used to a very private lifestyle and neither of us really wants an intruder—and I should have figured out months ago that you needed me to make the offer, Bett. So if it's tough going, it's tough going. Families are still the only people you can count on in time of trouble. I ought to know; I hadn't had any family for a long time until I met you. And I refuse to let you worry about Liz long-distance any longer." Zach paused, a wry grin on his lips. "Am I the only one having this conversation?"

"No." Bett smiled, trying to relax. It was so typical of Zach to take the bull by the horns. And it was typical of him to give willingly of himself to please her. Tiny knots were forming in the pit of her stomach at the thought of having her mother here, day in, day out, but she ignored them, a wave of love for Zach overtaking any lesser emotions.

She smiled again, slid her arms around his waist, and hugged him. Zach smelled like sun and wind, an earthy, primitive scent that she loved. He rocked her close to him, his lips brushing her forehead.

"You weren't really afraid I'd nix the idea of inviting her here?" he murmured against her ear. "Lord, Bett, you didn't think I'd say no, just because we'd be a little inconvenienced for a time?"

"It wasn't you, Zach." Bett hesitated, staring at the hollow of his throat. "First, I felt . . . the thing is, Mom is still young; fifty-four is hardly ancient. I want to help her, yes, but she's always depended on other people, Zach, and I felt she needed to . . ." Bett groped for the words, " . . . get her life in order. For *her* sake. I was hoping that in time she'd make new friends on her *own*, come to some decisions, develop new interests. Her whole life's been devoted to taking care of people, and I . . ."

Zach nudged her chin up, a small surprised frown on his forehead. "So she depends on us for a while. That's not so terrible."

Bett took a breath. "No," she agreed hesitantly.

"Don't tell me you really don't want her here? That doesn't sound like you, two bits."

How could she be so ungenerous of spirit, when Zach was so very generous? What kind of inhuman, insensitive daughter wouldn't do anything to help her mother through a bad time? "Of course I want her here," Bett said vibrantly, and meant it. "Zach, it was so good of you to ask her . . ."

Zach drew back and kissed her on the nose. "Settled then?" he asked briskly.

"Yes," she agreed.

"Come on." He turned and pulled her toward the door. "We have a very serious problem on the back forty we need to take care of."

"Pardon?"

Bett was still in a distracted mood until she realized where Zach was driving. The landscape around the pond disclosed no problem that she could see. Night had fallen on the farm like black silk. It was still tropically warm, but the hush of evening was soothing, a stillness one could almost breathe in. Crickets chirped in the cattails, and the fragrance of ripening peaches was a thick, sweet perfume that filled the air.

Zach turned off the ignition and just looked at her, his face half in shadow, his eyes fathomless and dark. "There's a blanket in back." He gave her no chance to respond to that, reaching for her swiftly, tugging her close to him in that sweet darkness. His tongue slowly traced her lower lip, then her upper one. He dried the faint moisture with his fingertip. His touch was very gentle, very soft, very slow.

Bett half closed her eyes, willing a dozen vague anxieties to disappear from her mind. She'd wanted to be with him, and she'd wanted him—like this—all day.

Worries about her mother's visit had sabotaged those feelings; yet the simple intimacy of just being held gradually melted that tension. When Zach's mouth covered hers, a little more of that anxiety seemed to vanish. Zach, at times, could be very hard to resist. Zach, at times, could have some very strange powers over her. He could make her believe that there was nothing more important than this instant in time, nothing more important than the feel of his lips on hers. His kiss was hungry, very softly, sensually lustful. The last lingering tension ebbed away in slow motion. His lips seared hers in an intimate stamp of possession, and only when her body seemed to go limp did the pressure of his mouth slowly lessen.

He drew back, his finger seductively trailing the line of her jaw. "You have," he whispered, "thirty-two seconds to get outside and take your clothes off."

She wasted ten of those seconds getting out of the truck, and then dawdled away an awful lot of time watching him unfold the blanket. She was smiling as he spread the blanket on the tall grasses next to the pond. He loved that smile, would happily have done cartwheels to banish the pinched look around her eyes that had haunted her since her mother's call. Bett was so rarely moody. Given any chance at all, she squeezed the joy from life, and shared it.

Whatever anxiety she was feeling, they would handle it. At the moment, he just wanted to see the mischievous spark back in her eyes. He wasn't disappointed. He paused briefly to study his wife appreciatively. She was wearing an old yellow T-shirt of his; its shoulder seams flopped almost to her elbows, its hem barely covered her fanny, and not a bump of a breast showed in the folds of fabric. Her old jeans led down to bare feet. His lady was at her sexiest, nonetheless. Softness was the issue. The softness of silky yellow hair by moonlight, the soft pastel of the T-shirt, the softer glow of her skin.

He unbuttoned and pushed off her jeans himself, since she was being so damned slow. She raised her arms; he tugged off the T-shirt.

It was Bett's turn to watch when she'd settled on the blanket. Zach's profile was outlined against the night sky, and a shiver of anticipation raced down her spine. Zach was all dark gold, his chest smooth and sculpted, strength and control part of his body, part of his every movement. He tossed his shirt on the grass, then slowly slid his belt from its belt loops, facing her. When he unsnapped the single button on his jeans, the small sound seemed to echo crazily in the night. In a moment, he'd skimmed off the pants, and moved toward her in the darkness, naked and tall.

A primitive shudder trembled through her body and refused to stop. How could she ever have thought Zach could survive cooped up in an office? He belonged here with the woods behind him, the wind ruffling his hair, the earth close. During the day, Zach was often friend, always husband, and at any hour lover. At night Zach was mate, and the word connoted for Bett a very secret, primal facet to loving that she'd never understood before knowing him. Some wild creatures chose their mates for life. Zach always gave her that feeling when he came to her, that he would claim what was his, that he would protect as well as take, that he would possess at a level far more complex than just the sexual one.

She felt all of that as he slid down next to her. His skin was so cool. She felt surrounded by the sweetness of grass and darkness. His eyes locked on hers, and then traveled down, an appraisal of her nakedness that curled her toes, a slow caress of sight instead of touch. His head bent over her, and his lips closed first on one breast, then the other. Bett arched beneath him, her hands sliding down over the smooth, firm flesh of his back. His tongue flicked delicately on one nipple, and an involuntary whimpering sound emerged from her throat.

Zach stole that sound in a kiss that shared tastes they both knew well. Never, never well enough. The hunger was so very sweet, a secret rush of sheer pleasure that came from knowing exactly what Zach could do with his lips and hands and his body joined with hers. Her breath quickened; his grew harsh, and then his touch gentled. They drew apart a little. The first surge of passion gradually slowed as they both sought to prolong their sweet, warm night.

"Zach?"

"Hmm?" He shifted her on top of him, loving her slight weight and supple limbs, the husky breathlessness in her voice, the way those soft eyes suddenly lowered in impossible shyness.

"I love you, Mr. Monroe." Her heart felt full. Singing. Earlier worries hadn't disappeared; they didn't need to. Just being with Zach reminded her that they'd already handled their share of problems together, and would again. Moving, the farm, their money crisis . . . but Zach was always there.

Just as he was there now, vibrantly alive beneath her, warm and in control. He was very good at taking control. His delightfully lazy hand was languidly sifting through her hair as if he would be content to play sensual lover all night. The lower part of his body delivered other messages.

Her finger traced the line of his jaw and then subtly applied pressure so that he turned his head. She raised up a little. Her fingers brushed aside his thick hair, and then slowly her forefinger drew a line around the shell of his ear. Zach tensed beneath her. As she leaned up just a little further, the tips of her breasts grazed his chest and her tongue slipped inside the auricle of his ear.

Zach twisted his head convulsively. "You've been reading dirty magazines," he whispered.

"I have not." He wasn't smiling, but his eyes were full of laughter. She shook her head. "You will lie back and enjoy this," she said with mock severity. "You're supposed to like it. The male of the species is supposed to go stark raving mad when his ear is . . . um . . ."

"Tickled to death?" While he had a moment's advantage, he claimed both her hands and twisted to pin her body beneath him.

She savored the weight of him for a moment. That control of his was slipping; she could feel it in the increased tension in his legs, could see it in his eyes. "Now, it's possible I don't have the technique down to perfection."

"You have *all* the techniques down to perfection," he assured her. To hide his smile, he nuzzled his lips against her shoulder, his hand stroking down her side to the silken curve of her hip. The urge to make leisurely love to her all night was quickly deteriorating into the need to take her. Very soon. "So what else have you been reading?"

"Nothing." Fascinated, she watched the moon shoot silver into his hair, and reached out to touch it. His hair naturally curved around her fingers and she imagined moonbeams in the touch of him, delighted at the whimsical thought. "You used to read that kind of thing in college, you know," she pointed out absently.

"Dirty magazines? One or two. Until I met you, and realized all those women were lumpy." Firm, callused fingers ran down her sides, then closed on her bottom, cupping the soft flesh, kneading it as he leaned closer to whisper in her ear. "Now, what else?" he murmured. "Don't tell me you stopped reading when you came to ears."

She squirmed. He held her fast. "Zach, we've been married awhile," Bett said uncomfortably. "I don't want you to get bored. A lot of time I really don't see how anyone without a master's degree in acrobatics can do any of that stuff. I mean, who needs a perpetual charley horse?" Her eyes met his, suddenly serious. "But that's not to say . . . Zach, I don't want you ever, ever to think that if you want to try something . . ." Her breath caught in her throat again. "I just want to be sure you know that. That I will at least try. Anything you want . . ."

He'd stopped smiling. His blue eyes had turned dark, liquid, intense. "That goes two ways, little one. We will always try anything *you* want. But as for any fear of my being bored with you . . ."

Zach leaned over her, his lips first rubbing hers lightly, then homing in as he drew her close. She made a tiny sound at the luxurious pressure of his mouth, at the sweep of his hands up and down her bare flesh. Her response was instant, all-giving. That was Bett. They'd both freely experimented from time to time; intimacy was a complex thing. Play was part of that, but Bett's sweetness and freedom in loving were what made their nights special. Bored? It wasn't conceivable. He sought to show her that. His tongue savored the honeyed darkness of her mouth, the hollow of her cheek, the smooth, pearly feel of her teeth.

His palm curled around her breast, his thumb brushing back and forth across her nipple. So taut, so tender, that sensitive flesh. He knew Bett. He knew exactly what ignited her primitive side. The small, perfect breast that barely filled his palm changed with a certain touch, swelled and hardened; he could feel the ache inside her begin to build. Her breasts were unbelievably sensitive. So were her inner thighs, her bottom. A caress around her navel could annoy her, throw her off a building rhythm. Bett was easily distracted; even just an odd sound in the night, and she had to be wooed back into the mood. She could be quite distressed with herself when that happened.

He had no intention of letting anything distract or distress her tonight.

She'd been upset by the call from her mother, he knew that. More than Bett would ever know, Zach resented the thought of a third person coming to live with them. If he'd invited the problem, it was for Bett's sake; he knew they had the strength in their marriage to live through this. Still, he was used to having Bett all to himself. He wanted, needed, and counted on having Bett to himself.

Like now. Bett was here. A black night surrounded them; Bett was damned well on fire. So was he. When he leaned over her, she wrapped her legs around his waist, forcing that first thrust so deeply inside her that he swore he touched her soul. Or his.

3

BETT HAD BEEN trying to convince herself for the past
hour that the rain was only a drizzle. It wasn't easy.
Water was dripping from her matted lashes and dribbling
down her neck, her hair was slicked to her scalp, and
her T-shirt was wet even under the yellow slicker. It was
eleven o'clock on the first morning of September, and
nature couldn't have chosen a nastier time to get touchy.

They had an order for field-run peaches that wouldn't
wait; Zach was at the market with their plums; rain meant
nighttime spray duty; and their picking crew would have
been delighted to walk out right now—except that no
respectable Spanish-speaking gentleman would consider
leaving the orchard as long as a woman was still willing
to work her heart out in the pouring rain.

Bett brushed a wet hand through her sopping hair and
crouched down again on the flatbed truck. Three field
crates to go, and the order would be completed. Lupe's
eyes were shooting daggers at her. An hour before, Zach
had told her to go home and dry off, that Lupe would
handle the picking crew. But Bett hadn't left, and Lupe
clearly didn't know quite what to do. Zach's orders were
usually more than reasonable; Zach's wife wasn't.

Bett acknowledged that she had a tiny stubborn streak, but quality control was the issue. "Field run" meant their buyer was prepared to take their fruit direct from the orchard. They received less money for their peaches that way, but they also didn't have to go through the expense of sorting and packing and packaging. Which was fine, only Bett didn't like anything leaving the farm with the MONROE label on it that was less than perfect if she could help it. These peaches were close, all forty-seven crates of them behind her.

The last three crates were finally heaved up to the truck bed, and Bett glanced up from her sorting task. "We done," Lupe told her, and stabbed a forefinger in her direction. "You go tell Señor Monroe you been home awhile."

"Yes, Lupe." She silently and fervently thanked God for male chauvinists. The crew would surely have abandoned their task if there hadn't been the issue of the men outlasting a lone woman in the rain. She felt a wave of affection for the workers. They looked so darned rough . . . but she'd been offered four additional raincoats in the past hour, which rather said it all. As their trucks rumbled off down the back road in quick succession, Bett stood up to walk over to the last three crates of peaches. On the far hill, she spotted a sudden flash of pink.

The flash quickly resolved itself into a shocking-pink Lincoln, four years old, with a U-Haul behind it that sagged dangerously close to the ground. The farm road was constructed for slow-moving tractors; the Lincoln seemed to be approaching at the speed of sound. Its brakes were slammed on just inches from the back of her truck, about the same time Bett vaulted down from the truck bed, her tennis shoes squishing on the slippery wet earth.

A pink and mauve polka-dotted umbrella emerged from the car first, then a blouse in a vivid print of pink, orange, and chartreuse. Pink culottes were next, and, finally, a brand-new pair of pink tennis shoes—Elizabeth's concession to farm life. Bett took one look at her mother and swallowed hard, before extending outstretched arms.

"Mom! We weren't expecting you for another two days."

"Oh, darling, I just couldn't wait. I started to think about how hard you two kids work and how much I could help you. *Brittany.*" Elizabeth's eyes glowed with tears. "I just felt better than I have in months, knowing you needed me. Without your father, I've just..." The glow threatened to become an instant deluge.

Swiftly and instinctively, Bett ducked under the umbrella and wrapped her arms around her mother. The scent of lavender surrounded her, as familiar as the oatmeal cookies she'd been fed as a child. Good food, good sleep, good love, Elizabeth used to say. A billion times? Bett found herself laughing as the rain pelted down on both of them.

Elizabeth pulled back first, surveying her daughter up and down. "Brittany, you are a total mess, and soaking wet."

"And before *you* are, we'd better get you to the house. Everything will be fine, Mom, I promise you."

"You're so busy, you and Zach. I'm so terribly afraid I'm going to be in your way..."

"You're *not* going to be in our way. We both want you here, very much. Now, just follow the truck in."

Bett kept an eye on her mother in the rearview mirror as they drove toward the farmyard. At fifty-four, Elizabeth still had a relatively unlined face, brown hair worn in a short mass of permed curls, and a trim figure a little on the buxom side. Her smooth skin and doelike brown eyes reflected the life she had lived, that of a sheltered homemaker who wanted nothing more from life than to be a sheltered homemaker.

The circles under Elizabeth's eyes made Bett ache for her mother. Elizabeth hadn't known how to even begin coping when Chet died. After more than a year, she still didn't. If the constant tears had finally eased a little, Elizabeth was still at sea over balancing checkbooks and caring for the yard, taxes, what to do with her time. The smallest decisions still overwhelmed her, not because she lacked ability or intelligence, but simply because she really didn't want to change her lifestyle.

Nurturing was her specialty. Babies knew it; babies were capable of spotting Elizabeth in a crowded room and holding out their arms to be picked up. Bett couldn't remember a time when her mother had ever raised her voice.

Bett had raised her own voice quite often in adolescence. She remembered that period of her life with utter misery. Elizabeth had so badly wanted a daughter created in exactly her own image. She had traditional values concerning home and hearth and women's roles, all of which she'd tried desperately to ingrain in her daughter. It hadn't worked. The failures began with her name. Early on her father had nicknamed her "Bett," thank goodness. "Brittany" was intended to evoke the genteel grandeur of the Old World and a buxom lass with rosy cheeks who needlepointed and raised babies. "Brittany" only made Bett think of clumsy spaniels, which was about what she'd felt like as a child. In more recent times, she still hadn't developed into anything remotely resembling "buxom," didn't sew, and had yet to produce offspring. Her list of failures to fit the mold was ongoing. None of these "faults" was really so terrible; it was just that mothers and daughters were supposed to be close. Elizabeth and Bett weren't, though they both tried very hard. Bett believed herself at fault, yet with all her efforts had never been able to bridge the distance between them.

At the moment, though, old memories weren't in her mind. Protective feelings swamped her as she glanced once more in the rearview mirror before braking the truck in the farmyard. This time, Bett was determined she would come through for her mother. There would be no hurt feelings, no arguments, no impatience. Her mom needed help, and Bett had every intention of being there for her.

Still, her eyes settled uneasily on the U-Haul behind the Lincoln. How literally had Elizabeth taken Zach's invitation to "stay as long as you like"?

The moment Bett opened the back door of her mother's car, Sniper leaped into the car in a flurry of Persian fur, discovering her mother's canary cage instantly as if he'd sensed the birds from half a mile away. "Behave yourself for once," Bett hissed. The cat sprang to the top of the felt-covered cage, purring. Bett batted the animal down, and tried to work the cage out over a lopsided suitcase.

"Brittany?"

"Coming!" The canaries twittered; Sniper snaked out a paw and playfully clawed Bett's wrist, then tried to leap on top of the cage again as Bett finally maneuvered it out of the car.

Elizabeth was waiting at the door to remove the wrap and coo at the two yellow birds. "I should have asked you if I could bring them. If you mind, darling—"

"Of course not." Bett pushed her damp hair back from her forehead. "Tell me what you need to bring in immediately, Mom; the rest we'll get after the rain stops."

"I really think you should get out of those wet clothes first."

Bett shook her head, smiling. "It's warm-wet, not cold-wet. Really, it's okay."

"Well, as far as just the essentials go . . ."

The seven plants had to come in—they could catch cold in the rain. The base for the canary cage. Four suitcases. Elizabeth never traveled without her own reading lamp and pillow, nor the box of china that had been a wedding gift when she'd married Chet. Four shoeboxes full of coupons; Elizabeth planned to go shopping. Three afghans; it was no fun at all to work on just one at a time. Her rocker with the yellow velvet cushion. She always sat in that rocker before dinner. "You're irritated with me, aren't you, Brittany?" Elizabeth said hesitantly.

Panting and dripping, Bett dropped the next load of boxes on the floor. The couches were filled. "Of course not, Mom."

"Well, if you wouldn't mind just bringing in the presents, then. Brittany, you're already so very wet, but I could hardly come without presents, now could I? It's not every son-in-law who would be willing to put up with his wife's mother for any period of time. I don't want him to think I don't appreciate it; you know I love Zach."

Bett soon discovered that Elizabeth loved Zach worth a purple tie, three issues of *Penthouse,* a bottle of Johnny Walker, one package of fresh-frozen crab from Alaska, a tie clasp adorned with brass golf balls, and four dress shirts in various pastels. "You think he won't wear the powder-pink?" Elizabeth fretted.

"He'll love it," Bett lied without a qualm. Zach would wear a pink shirt when mainland China became a democracy—sort of a better-not-hold-your-breath kind of proposition. But Elizabeth was so pathetically eager to please . . . "Anything else we need this minute?"

"Just a few things," Elizabeth beamed delightedly as Bett brought in the last stack of boxes. "You can open them all later, Brittany, but just peek at that first one."

Bett dutifully opened the first box. A bright-green blouse with zigzaggy stripes and ruffles. She stared blankly.

"I thought it would make you look a little bustier, darling, no offense—you do like it?"

"It's lovely." Bett tried to sound enthusiastic.

"You don't like it." Elizabeth sounded hurt.

"Honestly, Mom, I love it." Bett swept back her hair again, swallowing a sigh. She tugged off the sopping yellow slicker. "Let's get you a cup of tea, now, shall we?" Quickly, she whisked the cat away from the birds again, nervously aware that her mother's critical eye was sweeping over the house. "Mom, since we weren't expecting you for another couple of days—"

"You think I've never seen a little dirt in my life?" Elizabeth naturally migrated toward the kitchen, Bett following. "This way I have something to do right off the bat. If I'd come later you'd have had the house spotless, now wouldn't you have?"

"Um, yes." If one didn't look in corners—which Elizabeth always did. "Mom, since you *are* early, I wasn't really sure which room you'd rather stay in. I know you usually stay in the spare room for a weekend, but for a longer stay I think you'd really be more comfortable on the main floor. Zach's study has a couch that opens into a really comfortable bed; there's a good closet, and it would be quieter for you . . ." And more private for everyone, though Bett would never have said it.

"Brittany. I wouldn't take Zach's study in a thousand years." Elizabeth bent down to reach under the sink. "You just go get out of those wet clothes, honey. I'll be fine. Don't you worry about me for a minute!"

"Mom. What are you *doing?"*

Elizabeth chuckled as she pulled out wastebasket, scouring powder, cleanser, and spare grocery bags from under the sink. "I might as well start by giving this floor a little lick and a promise. Won't take me a minute. Where's your toothbrush for the corners? I could have sworn I gave you a dozen last year."

Bett mentally counted to ten, skipping half the numbers. Not that she was in any way getting upset. She was going to start out by getting Elizabeth happily settled in and relaxed if it killed her. "Look, you just got here,"

Bett said cheerfully. "Couldn't we sit down for a minute? You've had such a long ride—"

"Brittany, I am *happy*. Although..." Elizabeth's lips pursed as she surveyed the kitchen. "I don't know that I can move the refrigerator alone. You know, your father always fitted our appliances with casters. I used to have terrible dreams about germs that multiplied—"

"*Mom.*"

"—under stoves and refrigerators. Nightmares. These invading armies of germs marching, marching, marching, threatening an entire family of little children..." She poured steaming tap water into a pail, then paused to frown at her daughter's choice of cleanser. "...*babies*. They could have *died* from those germs. I poured bleach on them in the dream. Gallons of it." She smiled blissfully at Bett. "I *love* a dirty floor. Yours is filthy, Brittany. I'm going to have such a good time here. Thank goodness Zach is different from your father, though; Chet would have had a *fit* if I kept a floor like this. Have you given up those wretched bees yet, sweetheart?"

"No," Bett said helplessly. Her mother had been here all of fifteen minutes and already she felt undermined. Guilty for the state of the house, for her inadequate figure, for her kitchen floor. And in disgrace because of the bees.

"And we'll have it all done before Zach comes in to dinner. He'll be pleased. Brittany, it is *not* necessary for you to help. Honestly, I am perfectly happy—"

"I know you are, Mom." Only Bett couldn't very well stand there and stare down at her mother, who was on her hands and knees. If Elizabeth wouldn't get up, Bett was obviously going down. On hands and knees, the two women faced each other, both smiling. Elizabeth's smile was delighted. "You know, we're going to have such a good time together!"

"Yes," Bett agreed. There was a semi due in for the peaches. The workers were expecting their paychecks.

She was freezing cold and her yellow shirt was sticking to her. They were going to have to spray tonight because of the rain, and it would take hours to unpack the rest of Elizabeth's U-Haul.

At another level, Bett felt a rush of warmth flood her at Elizabeth's smile. Those smiles had been all too rare this last year. Okay, Mom, Bett thought fleetingly. I am not going to feel irritated. We are going to be *calm* together. And I am darned well going to keep you happy or die trying. She picked up the scrub brush.

Zach strode impatiently toward the house. The entire day was a bitch. Six hours of spraying coming up, *not* his favorite chore. He hadn't liked leaving Bett with a crew in the rain, and in the meantime the semi had just arrived, with Caruso's Mercedes trailing it. Their buyer always had an hour to spare for showing off pictures of his grandchildren. By spending time, Caruso seemed to feel he was "cultivating" one of his favorite growers. The only cultivating Zach had time for during the harvest season was in a field, and he still had miles to go this day. Bett usually handled Caruso, but Zach had seen the pink Lincoln in the yard, the one Chet had paid God knows how much to have custom-painted some years back.

A warm, wet muzzle snuggled into Zach's palm; he paused long enough to stroke the oversized, mangy beast to whom it belonged. "Baby" was one of Bett's orphans. The thin line of Zach's mouth softened. He crouched down on his haunches. "So where've you been, you old cuss? Bett's been worried."

The dog moaned at the sound of Bett's name. Zach chuckled, stroking the bristly fur under the animal's chin one last time. Bett had her bees. The cat. A fawn she'd managed to charm into the backyard last winter. She'd trained a covey of pheasants to come to the back door to be fed on snowy days. And the pigeons that made a disastrous mess on the barn roof were "homers"—which meant they were supposed to go *home*. Instead, they had a cooing fit whenever Bett set foot outside.

His wife was fey. Baby, the mangy mutt, was just a part-time visitor who'd limped up to the door one day with a trap caught on one paw. The dog somewhat resembled a Great Dane, but with a hound's sagging jaws and a setter's sweeping tail. He checked in regularly with Bett, just wouldn't stay. Zach wondered fleetingly how Bett had ever thought herself happy as a city girl. His love for wild creatures matched hers, but he didn't have her special gift with them.

Just an appreciation for it. He stroked the dog's head one last time. "She'll be out," he promised, and made for the house.

Chaos greeted him at the door. Boxes and grocery bags and suitcases were piled every which way; the two canaries were chittering with fright. Sniper, who never came inside, was perched on top of the cage, interestedly batting his paw between the gold bars. Used to coolness and silence when he walked into the house, Zach swallowed a sigh of exasperation and made his way along a hazardous path toward the kitchen.

His nose wrinkled instantly at the smell of ammonia; after that jarring note came another. There was a feminine screech the moment his booted foot hit the floor; for some unknown reason the refrigerator was in the middle of the room; and before he had a chance to draw a breath, his mother-in-law was hurling herself at him.

He not only accepted the quick hug, he returned it; but he didn't have much chance to greet her.

"I wanted so much for us to have it done before you came in!" Elizabeth said unhappily. "Zach, I'm so glad to see you! I've brought you a few things—listen, you just sit down. I'll get you some iced tea. In the living room, there's no walking on the kitchen floor just yet.

Not that you can't if you want to," she added hastily. "It's just that—"

"You're looking great, Liz," he interjected as soon as she stopped to draw breath. His exasperation faded a little. He really was pleased to see the animated enthusiasm on his mother-in-law's face, and he would undoubtedly find the patience to listen to her steady stream of chatter once he got his business taken care of. Elizabeth was just—Elizabeth.

He refused the offer of iced tea three times, listened to the story of her drive from Milwaukee, stood obediently in the doorway, gathered after several hurt looks that he was supposed to comment on the floor and did so dutifully, and finally got a word in. "Where's Bett?"

Elizabeth motioned vaguely toward the refrigerator. "But you're *sure* I can't get you some coffee, then?" she asked worriedly. "Zach, you work so hard; you must need a little refreshment..."

He shook his head, took a step toward the freestanding refrigerator, and stopped at the expression of horror on Elizabeth's face. He stepped back, pushing off one boot and then the other. On stockinged feet, he ventured in, past the pail and rag, around the corner of the refrigerator. If he hadn't spotted the crown of yellow hair, he would have kept on going. As it was, he paused in shock and leaned over the counter.

Bett was trapped between the back of the refrigerator and the wall. She looked up at him from on her hands and knees, a toothbrush in one hand.

"What the Sam *Hill* are you doing?" he mouthed.

"Hi," she mouthed back. She was damp, hot, frustrated, and irritable... but the bewildered look on Zach's face almost made her chuckle. She made motions to show what she was doing—the toothbrush, the small bowl of pasty-looking cleanser and water, and the corner—and shot him a mischievous grin. "Zach, you *know* I always clean behind the refrigerator once a week," she said aloud.

"Hmm," he commented noncommittally, and reached down as she reached up for a quick kiss. "Caruso's out there. He claims he told you he wanted twenty more bushels."

She grinned again. "He always says that when the produce is good. It usually means he's irritated that he didn't order more because he knows he can sell it. You told him you always wanted that Mercedes of his?"

Zach looked blank. "No."

"And the grandchildren, Zach. He talks about the grandsons, but it's the granddaughter who's the apple of his eye. And after that, you mention that Joe Cranston offered you a quarter more per bushel than he did."

Zach heaved a sigh. "Two bits, who the hell is Joe Cranston?"

Bett shook her head sadly. "Sweetheart," she said with exasperation, "Joe Cranston is a figment of my imagination, of course. I swear, Zach, you're incurably honest."

And Bett, Zach thought idly, was incurably winsome. Her rainwashed hair had dried in a flyaway halo; her small frame was tucked quite comfortably into that tiny square; and the blue eyes staring up at him were clearly inviting. "Come out of there and say that," he suggested threateningly.

"You two," Elizabeth said affectionately. Zach straightened up, only to see his mother-in-law swabbing at his footprints with a rag. Guiltily, he backed up, and by the time he reached the doorway, Elizabeth was handing him his boots.

"I want to talk to you before you go back to work," she whispered as they walked toward the front door. "Zach, I . . . I'm very grateful you were willing to ask me here. I want to tell that I'll be very, very careful not to get in your way. I want you and Brittany to just go on and do things exactly as you always do . . ."

Elizabeth was on the eccentric side; she could also be

a sweetheart. Zach gave her a hug, reassured her, made a token stab at guessing the hour he would be in for dinner, and escaped outside. He found himself thankful gulping in a lungful of fresh air. He *hated* the smell of ammonia.

The incongruous picture of Bett cleaning behind the refrigerator brought a wry grin for a minute . . . but the grin faded. He'd already urged Bett to do whatever she had to do to make her mother's transition to the house easier, and to forget about the farm. In his mind, though, he had anticipated a break for Bett, and had hoped that Elizabeth might take on some of the household jobs that exhausted his wife at the end of an already tiring workday. Liz loved housework, and she wanted to be needed. Inviting her had seemed an honest exchange of needs.

Let them be, Zach thought absently. After all, Elizabeth had only been there an hour. If he felt a sudden trace of uneasiness, it was merely because he was already feeling tired and exasperated. Caruso was waiting.

4

"Do you like it, Zach?" Elizabeth asked worriedly. "I made it especially for you."

"Wonderful, Liz. Really." Zach viewed the slice of salmon loaf on his plate with a haunted smile. Elizabeth had served the dish the first night she was here, and to please her, he had complimented her on it. Five days later, it was being served again, now that she had established it as his favorite.

Bett tossed him just a wisp of an unholy smile. She knew Zach hated salmon. He served himself another helping of green beans. Picking up her fork again, Bett stifled a yawn.

Plum harvest had just started. With both peaches and plums going on at the same time, she barely had time to breathe, even if Zach took on the brunt of the work. In the meantime, she'd spared every free minute she could for her mother . . . and that included, so far, every single evening. Elizabeth did her best worrying after midnight, after she'd tried to go to sleep and discovered that the house was too quiet.

Now, everything was going well, Bett told herself. Just as she'd been telling herself regularly since the minute her mother had arrived. The two women were getting along splendidly, better than they ever had before. There had been no friction, none of Elizabeth's tearful crying bouts; her mom's face had taken on color and animation. Everything Bett wanted for her mother had been happening. And Zach must have told her a dozen times that it was an ideal arrangement, that she should just stop worrying about the farm work that wasn't getting done and spend as much time with her mother as she wanted.

It would have been very selfish indeed to admit that anything was bothering her. The canaries cheeping at five in the morning didn't bother her. The fact that making love with Zach had been interrupted twice by their resident insomniac didn't bother her. Coming home after seven straight hours in the orchards to wash ceilings with her mother didn't bother her. Her mother's delicate suggestions that ruffles and padded bras and makeup "would help" didn't bother her.

Nothing bothered her. Not even tonight. Bett was close to being slaphappy tired. And Zach hadn't even guessed that something odd was afoot, even though her mother was sitting there in a black linen dress.

Zach viewed his mother-in-law with increasingly suspicious, though hooded, eyes. Elizabeth favored colors that verged on fluorescent. *Not* black. Elizabeth automatically spent every entire dinner period chattering. Yet tonight she was reasonably silent.

He hardly knew what to do with the peace.

"Are you going out to work after dinner, Zach?" Elizabeth asked idly.

"For a while. Just to tinker with a carburetor for a short time." Not long. Bett's eyes had shadows under them. Since his wife, for some strange reason, had given up sleeping this last week, he was determined to get her into bed at a reasonable hour. For one purpose or another. The pale yellow smock she wore had long sleeves and an open throat; she looked feminine and tiny and delectably touchable. In the meantime, she and her mother exchanged swift glances.

Elizabeth rose, reaching for the empty plates. "Well, if you have to work after dinner, you have to, I guess, Zach."

"Hmm." That was not the tune she'd been singing previously. Elizabeth had been meeting him at the door with iced tea and long, ego-boosting monologues about how hard he worked, how strong he was, and how much he needed a little spoiling. He'd sponged it up, the first two days. By the third day, he was thanking God that Bett was nothing like her mother.

"You two aren't planning on going anywhere after dinner, are you?" he asked idly.

Bett lurched up from her chair; Elizabeth shot him a startled look. "What on earth makes you say that?" his mother-in-law asked with a little laugh. "I'm going to get you your coffee now, Zach, and if you want some dessert—"

"No, thanks—honestly, Liz. I'm more than full."

"Well, there are eclairs in the refrigerator for whenever you want them. I made them especially for you; Bett told me how you—"

"Thank you. *Where,*" Zach said patiently, "were you two planning on going?"

"I'll be right back," Bett promised from the doorway, and disappeared.

Elizabeth glanced at the empty doorway with a sour expression. "We were just going for a little drive."

"Anywhere special?"

"Can't hear you," Elizabeth told him over the rush of both water faucets at the sink.

"Anyplace special?"

"Still can't hear you. Could it wait until I get the dishes done, Zach? Oh, your coffee..."

"No need," Zach said quietly, which Elizabeth heard just fine.

He found Bett inside the closet in their bedroom, bending over as she slipped into a pair of heeled sandals. Sniper was lounging on the buttercup-yellow spread; Zach scooped the cat up, plopped him outside the bedroom door, and closed it.

Bett stiffened at the sound of the door closing. She gave one quick glance at the interesting scowl between her husband's brows and went back to fastening the second sandal. "Now, just don't ask. You'll be happier."

"I'm happy enough."

She shook her head, straightening up. "You have that 'difficult' look on your face."

"What I *have* is a strong inclination to put you to bed. You've been burning the candle at both ends for the better part of a week."

"I've got energy coming out of my ears," she assured him. She flashed him a smile as she crossed swiftly to the dresser. She picked up a hairbrush and rapidly restored her hair to order, unobtrusively glancing worriedly at the mirror at the same time. Did she really look so tired that he noticed? she wondered.

Behind her, the sunset was pouring pastel rays through the windows on either side of their double bed. The vaulted ceiling and huge domed windows were Zach's designs. Her choices were the gentle yellow color of the carpet and fabrics, and closets that had enormous mirrors on the doors. Nasty things to clean, those mirrors, but then a few candles and darkness and bare skin and those mirrors—and Zach—could produce a remarkable number of variations on a theme . . .

"Is there some particular reason you don't want to tell me what's going on?" his baritone growled behind her.

"Of course there is," Bett said cheerfully. Finally, her hair lay silken and still on her shoulders. She set down her brush. "You wouldn't approve." Spraying on a quick whiff of perfume, she turned. "For no good reason. Not to worry."

"Then why am I worried?"

"Now, we're giving you a perfect chance to put your feet up in peace for an evening," Bett teased, but her light tone was at total variance with the sudden rush she made for the door. Zach had to be faster than lightning to catch her, but suddenly his hands were at her waist and the door was behind her. Her husband had the magical ability to appear huge at will. The whole range of her vision was filled with his short-sleeved navy-blue sweat shirt. The chest it covered wasn't remarkably different from the door in terms of flexibility.

She tilted up her head and looked into Zach's eyes. A whole bluer than blue sky couldn't have been that full of laughter. She considered making another escape attempt, but didn't have the chance before he placed a kiss on her mouth. The kind designed to remind her that it had been far too long since they had last made love. "Lord, you're a tease," he murmured.

She was the tease? He'd refined the practice since they'd been married. His tongue slipped between her parted lips and sought hers. Ever so gradually, a steady, unconscious tension that had gripped her for days relaxed; a languid weariness flowed through her body. His tongue continued to play a game of thrust and parry, very gentle, very provocative. No hurry, said the movements of Zach's tongue, as if something inside him was quite aware she'd been leading the life of a racehorse all week.

When Zach took over, he took over. The race was over, and she found slow motion infinitely preferable to fast. Her fingertips slowly walked up his forearms, up the soft material covering his shoulders, up and into his hair. He seemed to like that quite well, because when he finally came up from the first kiss for air, on the inhale he was already dipping down for the second. That one lasted until he'd thoroughly mussed her hair and run his hands all the way down to her bottom and back up again. Bett was clinging to him, rubbing her hips in a most private rhythm against his hard thighs. Zach flicked open the collar of her dress to press a kiss against her collarbone. "Now, where is it you're certainly *not* going?" he murmured idly.

"To a psychic," Bett answered, and leaned her cheek into his shoulder. She felt Zach stiffen, and sighed. "I had a feeling you heard me," she said dryly. "Mom read this card on the bulletin board in the grocery store two days ago and called the guy. He reads...'auras.' She's decided to...um...have a little chat with Dad."

Zach very definitely pulled back then. "Let's hear that again?"

Bett's hands fluttered in the air. Anxiety darkened her eyes, but at the same time a hint of humor softened the curve of her lips. "Mom...she seems to feel it's about time she let go of grieving, which you know I'd do anything to help her with! But she's so set on this idea. She figured that one last chance to contact Dad—"

"When exactly did your mother lose her mind?"

"Be nice," Bett coaxed.

"I'm being *very* nice."

"Zach, she is *going*. Now, there's no talking her out of it; I tried. And obviously I couldn't let her go alone. The Lord knows what she'd get herself into..." Bett caught her breath. "It'll probably be fun. Ghosts and levitation and stuff..."

Zach pushed back his hair with a thoroughly perplexed frown. He held back the expletive on the tip of his tongue. Bett was so tired she could barely stand up straight, but her eyes stared determinedly up at him. Lord, she was a stubborn little minx! "So how much is the resident ghost hunter taking her for?" he asked flatly.

"I don't know. Neither does she. Mom doesn't care." Bett clearly did.

"You want me to talk to her?"

"If I thought it would do any good, I'd say yes. Unfortunately, I really believe she'd just sneak off to him sometime when she thinks we don't know about it, and then I would worry—"

"Yes." He had the measure. Bett had been roped in. She didn't need anyone giving her a hard time. His eyes held hers, half filled with humor. "If there are black candles and they ask for a show of hands for a virgin sacrifice, *don't* volunteer." His half-smile died when she didn't return it. "How bad can it be, some guy who advertises in a grocery store?" he asked wryly.

"Mmm." Bett chewed on her lower lip, and moved out of his arms to reach for the brush again. Zach had no appreciation for hairstyles. He was a toucher. "That isn't exactly why I thought you wouldn't approve of the idea."

"What *exactly* is the part I'm supposed to object to?"

"Nothing, really." It was just the place they were going. Kind of a rural slum on the edge of nowhere, the tag end of a poor farming community about twenty miles away. Anyone with a suicide wish could wander around there at night without any problem. "I'm sure its reputation is vastly overrated. So it's a poor area. Zach, that doesn't necessarily mean—"

"Oh, no. But I should have guessed where the local psychic would hang his shingle."

Unsmiling, Zach pulled off his sweat shirt and reached into the closet for a short-sleeved blue shirt.

"Zach, you don't have to go. Really."

Buttoning his shirt, he was inclined to take both women over his knee. The older one for a spanking. The other one to cuddle up.

Pushing the gearshift into neutral, Zach leaned forward and peered through the windshield. The pitch-black gravel road had never seen a streetlamp. A single swaying lantern creaked back and forth over a peeling sign that read:

REVEREND MOODY, SPIRITUALIST
PSYCHIC READINGS
Séances   Healings
Appointment Only

He and Bett exchanged a dry glance. There wasn't
much they could tell from the exterior of the ranch house;
it was too overgrown by shrubbery and low-hanging trees
to get a good look at it. Bett had relaxed from the time
she knew Zach was coming along, but the mood was
still rather eerie. A chill had touched the back of her
neck and was more than ready to travel up and down her
spine at a moment's notice. Zach couldn't have been less
affected, as he matter-of-factly leaned over the back seat
with a carefully serious expression on his face.

"Listen, Liz. No need for all of us to go in, now is
there? You two stay in the car; I'll just pop in there
and...um...talk to Chet, and then—"

"Oh, no, Zach. I've talked to the Reverend Moody
three times in the last two days, and I definitely have to
be there. I thought you knew all about psychic spirits?
When you said you were coming, you told me how interested you'd always been—"

"Mmm," Zach grumbled as he cut the engine and
jerked out of the car. Opening the door for his mother-
in-law, he watched Elizabeth dart out and start up the
dark, winding path, as excited as a little kid, her hands
firmly clasped in front of her. Exasperation warred with
humor inside of him.

Bett slipped an arm around Zach's waist, glancing up
at him as they strolled up the walk. "You're really irritated, aren't you?"

He squeezed her shoulder. "Not at you." A hiss and
a snarl from the front porch made Bett stiffen in alarm.
"A black cat," he murmured under his breath. "Why am
I not surprised?"

Bett relaxed again. "Behave yourself," she mouthed, her lips twitching with laughter.

"Are you kidding? I *am*," he mouthed back.

Reverend Moody was already greeting Elizabeth at the door. He was a gray-haired man with a long face, soulful eyes, and a black suit that was just a touch shiny in the seat. He chattered to Elizabeth as if he'd just found a long-lost friend, eyed Bett at length from head to toe, and wasted a fleeting disappointed look as he registered Zach's presence.

By the time the "so glad you're here" stuff was over with, the three of them were inside. "Perhaps a slight libation to relax all of us before we begin," the reverend suggested soothingly as he led them through a carpetless hall, lit only faintly by a dangling light bulb.

"Thanks, but we're not much into libations, Reverend," Zach said pleasantly. "Before we go any further, though, I wonder if I could have a private word with you."

"Certainly, certainly."

First, Zach took a cursory look at the room into which Reverend Moody was ushering the two women. It was square and dark, lit only by candles, and held a circular table in the center of it, covered, not surprisingly, with a black tablecloth. Harmless. Bett shot him a startled look, but he closed the door on her and faced the reverend without any more smiles.

"How much?" he demanded flatly.

"I sense," the tall man said soothingly, "a slight skepticism, which I assure you I have encountered before. Once you've seen—"

"I'm sure," Zach agreed. "How much?"

The reverend shook his head sadly. "A really very nominal contribution." He cleared his throat. "Twenty-five dollars."

Zach dug into his pocket, handed the man his fee,

and leveled him an iceberg stare. "Rev? Just so we both know what I'm paying for. You lay any hocus-pocus on those two, and I guarantee you'll have a real vision of the spirit world—direct. Got it?"

"Sir—"

"And you'll also see that Mrs. Cordell gets enough out of this *experience* that she will have absolutely no need ever to return here. *Ever*. Now, are we clear on that, too?"

"You may just be surprised with what the spirit world can come up with, Mr. Monroe," the Reverend Moody said acidly. Under Zach's steely stare, he turned away. "I think we're all very clear on what to expect this evening."

Bett felt a zigzag of apprehension tickle her spine as the door opened and Zach finally returned with Reverend Moody. The whole room, the whole house and grounds, gave her the creeps. Rationally, she knew very well that the "Reverend," though no man of the cloth, was only a harmless character and that there was nothing to be afraid of. In college, she'd even fooled around with ESP, a fascinating experience. But this was different. Her brain seemed to be functioning at only half the speed of the pulse beating in her throat. *Cobwebs* was what this place suggested to her—she felt as though they were going to cover her head any minute and smother her. She couldn't really shake the idiotic feeling until Zach sat down rather heavily beside her and laid a possessive hand on her thigh.

The reverend sat down, took Elizabeth's hands in his own, and stared deeply into the lady's eyes for several silent minutes. "I sense," he said slowly, "the most wonderful, loving aura around you, Mrs. Cordell . . ."

After a time, Bett's spine gradually unglued from the back of the straight chair. The Rev really wasn't so bad; she was even beginning to be rather taken by his low, sonorous voice. He was actually very comforting, in a spooky sort of way.

He related a number of incidents in the life of her mother and father that he could not possibly have known—if, that is, Bett weren't already aware that Elizabeth had spent time on the phone with him. Her mother seemed suspended in that world of wanting to believe. Bett felt a rush of protective love for her... but it wasn't necessary. The reverend wasn't doing any harm.

He claimed Chet loved Elizabeth and would always love her, that he wanted her to be happy. That he would be waiting for her in another world, but in this one he wanted his wife to take up the reins of life again, even to find someone else to love...

Elizabeth stiffened indignantly at that.

Bett didn't. Her dad, who would have deplored this whole scene almost as much as Zach did, would probably have offered those same words, and meant them. The reverend went on a little longer, surprising Bett when he assured Elizabeth that Chet didn't need to talk with her again through any medium when he was always in her heart. Didn't the rev count on repeat visits for his money? Bett was even more surprised when he finished with her mother and, before she could rise from the table, grasped both *her* hands.

"Oh, really, this isn't necessary. I—"

"There's a spirit calling you, too, Mrs. Monroe," the Reverend Moody said soothingly. "All you have to do is relax and let it happen."

"I am relaxed, thank you, but I—"

"Brittany," her mother hissed scoldingly.

Bett sighed.

The reverend's eyes focused dead behind her on Zach for one long, level moment before they closed. "A living, loving spirit," said the low seductive undertone. "Someone from your past. A lover? Yes, I think a past lover, Mrs. Monroe..."

Bett stiffened as if she'd been doused with ice water. What *else* had her mother told the reverend in those phone calls? And actually, Elizabeth couldn't have *known* that when Bett was eighteen...

"A long time ago...before this marriage...it's one of the strongest auras I've ever felt, Mrs. Monroe. It's a man—I'm trying to picture him—a very tall, very handsome young man. The two of you were so very young, so very much in love, so very eager to explore all the meanings of love together. I see long, blissful nights of passion. I see him taking you in his arms that first time—"

Zach's chair scraped behind her. Her right hand was plucked from the reverend's grasp, then her left one. "Thanks so much, Rev," Zach said crisply. "We're leaving now."

Bett considered mentioning that Andrew had hardly been "very tall" and that the reverend certainly had enough creative imagination to sell swampland in Arizona. After one glance at Zach's face, though, she decided it just wasn't the right time.

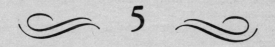

5

"A LOT OF NONSENSE, really," Elizabeth said virtuously. "I knew that ahead of time. You don't think I didn't?"

"Of course you did," Bett agreed.

"You think I needed some stranger to tell me your father loved me?"

"No, Mom," Bett agreed.

"And what a shyster he was, with all that business implying you weren't a virgin when you married. Honestly, Brittany! I remember now that he asked me on the phone all about the family, and maybe I even mentioned Andrew's name, heaven knows why. I know I can get to talking on occasion...but I certainly *never* would have intimated such a thing. I know perfectly well you were a good girl when you married Zach..."

Bett removed her tongue from her cheek long enough to reply, "Yes, Mom." The last one in, she closed the front door and dropped her purse and sweater on the couch. Zach was already heading upstairs. He had barely said a word the entire drive home, not that he wasn't exhausted. After working a twelve-hour day, he'd needed that ridiculous outing like a hole in the head. It was after midnight, and no wonder he was a bit...taciturn.

It undoubtedly had nothing at all to do with that slight oversensitivity he'd always had on the subject of one Andrew Alexander.

"Brittany, wouldn't you like to have a cup of tea with me before we go to sleep?" Elizabeth paused hopefully in the doorway to the kitchen.

"Honestly, not tonight." Bett gave her mother a hug and a smile. "I'm really bushed, and the alarm will be ringing at five-thirty."

"Maybe I should go to bed then, too," Elizabeth said absently.

"Good idea."

"Is it supposed to be nice tomorrow? I didn't hear a weather report after dinner."

Bett put one foot on the stairs. "Good night, Mom." One could get drawn into these rambling conversations for an endless period of time. Elizabeth could discuss for up to an hour whether or not she wanted to go to bed. Bett understood; night was the loneliest time, the time when Elizabeth missed her husband most, the time when she needed someone close to her. Tonight, though, she was stuck with a daughter who felt somewhere between old-rag tired and porcupine edgy.

"Maybe I should work on one of the afghans for a while. If I don't get started, they'll never get done." Elizabeth peered up at her daughter at the top of the stairs.

Bett turned the corner out of sight, that slight prick of guilt gnawing inside the way it always gnawed when she failed her mother, even in the littlest things. Behind the closed door of the bathroom, she washed her face, tugged off the smocked dress, and tossed it in the wicker laundry bin. To accuse her mother of selfishness was absurd, when the lady would positively break her back to "do for" and please her loved ones. But it *did* seem that Elizabeth always needed something from Bett, and Bett hadn't stopped feeling drained for a week.

The door to the master bedroom was closed. Silently, Bett turned the knob and tiptoed into the dark room wearing only her bra and half-slip. Zach had crashed; she could see his long frame sprawled on the bed in the shadows. Slipping off the rest of her clothes, she slid slowly down between the cool sheets. The mattress and pillow cushioned her weary body. For a moment, she lay on her back, and then instinctively turned, sliding an arm around Zach's waist to cuddle next to him.

It was difficult to cuddle next to steel.

Zach, though totally still and silent, was not asleep. Every muscle from his neck to his spine could have won an award for stiffness. Since he hadn't said anything, Bett knew he didn't want to talk. She hesitated unhappily. There were times to give a mate space, and times when that space only made things worse. After putting in the grueling workdays he'd been putting in, and after a fiasco like the evening just past, Zach was certainly entitled to a little "let me alone" time. Only she had the feeling he was annoyed by something completely different.

She leaned back a little, staying on her side. Slowly, with an almost imperceptible touch, her palms smoothed up Zach's back and her fingers curled on both sides of his neck. His muscles actually tightened at her touch. She paid no attention. Letting the heels of her hands rest on his bare shoulders, she pressed her fingers lightly around his collarbones, her thumbs rubbing gently into the nape of his neck and his scalp.

Gradually, her eyes became accustomed to the darkness, to the black and white and gray of moonlight. Her hands looked very white next to Zach's dark skin, a sensuous contrast. Her gentle touch turned bolder, as she massaged muscles that didn't want to unknot, concentrating on his most vulnerable spots, absorbed in the challenge. Her fingertips slowly took on the warmth of his skin and fed it back to him. As the knots smoothed out, her own tension eased and turned into lazy pleasure at the touch of him. She tested the effectiveness of her treatment with her forefinger. She pushed just slightly at his back; he immediately collapsed on his stomach. Zach was a disgraceful sucker for a back rub.

Silently, she tugged the sheet off altogether and straddled his back, feeling a thousand totally sexual nerve endings tingle with interest at the feel of her bare thighs against his bare hips. It was so very dark. Barely a hint of moonlight strayed in through the windows; not a sound intruded in the still room. Her hands rubbed and kneaded and smoothed. Arching forward, she massaged his shoulders, the tips of her breasts gently teasing the smooth skin of his back. Then she worked down, vertebra by vertebra, her legs tightening around his hips in natural balance as she moved. Her hands seemed to become part of his skin, and when she heard his groan of pleasure she smiled, but didn't stop.

Only when she was certain every tendon had gone limp, every muscle had relaxed, did her fingertips change their rhythm to a slow caress of circles and butterfly patterns.

"About a hundred years ago," she whispered lazily, "I understand that a woman used chicken blood to convince a lover that he was the first." She traced the line of his spine with a long, gentle finger. "I don't think they sell it at the drugstores nowadays."

Even in the darkness, she could see his thick black lashes flutter upward. So he thought she didn't know what was bothering him? She leaned forward, letting her nipples rub back and forth between his shoulder blades.

"So maybe I never should have told you about Andrew? Or maybe you shouldn't have asked. How was I to know it was going to bother you so much?" Her lips pressed tightly on the nape of his neck, then trailed along the curl of his shoulder in a series of very light kisses. "Or I could have told you he was a bastard. That the sex was dreadful." Bett took a breath, and then let her tongue erase all those little kisses on the way back to his neck. "Loving with you is perfect, you know. There isn't any comparison, and never has been. But I refuse to lie to you, Zach, out of... pride. Yes, I had another relationship, and it was a very good one. I grew up because of it; I was ready to learn what love was and what I wanted from a relationship because of it. Without Andrew, Zach, the two of us might never have been. So if you expect me to be ashamed of what happened before I even met you—"

One instant Bett was perched on his back and the next she was sprawled beneath him. Amazingly, Zach no longer had the lazily relaxed qualities of a man ready for sleep. Something very definitely alive and unyieldingly firm was pressing against her abdomen. Zach's skin was warm and vibrant, and his mouth anchored on hers, interrupting her speculative monologue. Her arms slid lightly around his neck as she savored all the allure in that kiss, all the tender, sweet, intimate taste of her lover. Only after an age did his mouth lift from hers. "There are times you make me feel like a fool, Bett. So the old mountebank got to me," he grumbled softly. "Haven't you ever felt jealousy?"

Her fingers traced the line of his jaw. "Definitely. When I see a woman look at you in a certain way, I feel this ugly, smothering urge to lock you up out of harm's way. And when I think of women you slept with before we met, I could paint my fingernails emerald. But, Zach, it's not the same."

He raised some of his weight from her by balancing on his elbows, his lips still dipping down to her nose, her cheek, into her hair. "*How* is it not the same when I feel jealous of you?"

"Because I don't want you to."

His smile pressed on her smile in a lazy kiss. "Two bits, that isn't rational."

"So?"

Zach's laughter rumbled from deep in his chest. He drew her closer to him, holding her tight, engulfing her with his warmth. His leg slid between hers as they rolled to their sides. The motion was intimate, their change of mood mutual. Bett's breasts swelled against him, aching as his palm possessively captured one sensitive orb.

She nearly jumped to the ceiling when she heard the gentle tap on the door. The door opened just a crack, about the time the top sheet was hurriedly being rustled into place.

"Brittany?" Elizabeth whispered. "Don't wake Zach, darling. I figured you wouldn't be asleep just yet..."

She couldn't find her crochet hook. Surely Bett had seen it? And in the meantime, Bett used to stock cinnamon tea; Elizabeth had looked all over the kitchen...

Bett rose, grabbed her robe, and belted it around her on the way downstairs. A half hour later, she returned to bed. Zach was still awake, but the mood was clearly broken. Exhaustion claimed both of them as she curled at his side.

"Bett?" Zach murmured just before sleep overcame them.

"Hmm?"

"Your mother is a very nice lady."

"Hmm," Bett responded again.

"That's the third time this week that she's prevented her daughter from being ravished. Now, is it me, or does she have ESP?"

Bett smiled, her eyes closed. "Zach, when she gets ...lonely, she just doesn't think. That, and I wouldn't be an acceptable member of the family if I didn't have insomnia."

"Try that again."

"My mother has insomnia. So did her mother; so did *her* mother; so did *her* mother; ad infinitum. Obviously, I have it, too. So she doesn't think she's waking me—"

"You've mentioned that you sleep like a brick?"

"No more than sixty-two times."

His arm draped lazily over her side, pulling her closer. "All right," he said sleepily after a time. "We'll live with it, regardless, Bett. Give or take her ridiculous psychic, she's a ton better. So we knew that a little disruption in our lives was inevitable. It won't kill us to live with it for a while."

Bett didn't answer, but simply curled closer to him. Zach, most of the time so very easygoing and patient, was unquestionably faring better through the "disruption" than she was. How could she feel disgruntled, when the problem was her own mother? She felt grateful that he wasn't angry over the interruptions in their love life. She felt resentful, as well, for her own sake. How *could* he not mind? *She* did.

Bett slipped a Debussy tape into the tape deck, let out the clutch, glanced in the rearview mirror of the tractor cab, and steered toward the orchard. A fine white cloud billowed from the spray rig behind her, covering tree after tree. The gentle strains of classical music didn't blend too badly with the soft whine of the sprayer.

Bett relaxed. The Massey was the best tractor they owned, and a beauty to work with. In the glass-windowed cab high above the ground, she was in her own private tower, loftily surveying the world she loved so well. She hummed an accompaniment to the rhythms around her. Every time one of the fledgling trees was covered, she felt a ridiculous surge of maternal relief. Got you, bug 9110. Safe, my sweethearts.

In college, she'd been an ardent ecologist; so had Zach. When they'd started farming, they'd made a solemn pledge not to use chemicals. They'd soon been forced to absolve each other of the pledge. No one wanted to buy wormy peaches. And there was no fun in watching a tiny tree one had planted, fed, watered, and nurtured with love wither because of a fungus.

She and Zach were careful with their chemicals, their idealism not so much lost as tempered with realism. Grady told them regularly they were fools to be so fussy. Grady, on the other hand, didn't view those rows of shiny green leaves and spreading branches as babies.

In two hours, she was done with the young block. There was another block to do in the afternoon, but it was almost lunchtime. Vaulting down the three steps of the tractor, Bett hopped to the ground, stuck her hands in her back pockets, and headed for the pickup.

She had left the driver's door of the vehicle open, on the off chance that Sniper wanted out. Sniper hadn't. In fact, the cat had picked up a hitchhiker, a saggy, tawny mutt with four inches of hanging jowls and mournful eyes.

"Baby!" A wet tongue lapped her cheeks as Bett hugged the hound. "So you're looking for a ride, are you?" Lap, lap, lap. Bett grimaced. "Would you mind washing the cat for a minute or two? You'll get your bone—you know there's no need to butter me up."

With a mournful sigh, Baby settled his head on Bett's lap, making it extra difficult to drive. She hadn't gone a hundred yards before she heard an odd sound in the engine. She braked to a stop, petted Sniper, shifted Baby's head, and stepped out to open the truck's hood. The fan belt had a habit of jumping off at will. Five years ago, Bett would have been collecting competitive bids from the local garages while waiting for a tow truck. But now, with a glove on one hand, she slipped the belt back in place and returned to the driver's seat.

The animals tussled for dominance, Sniper ending up on Bett's lap this time and Baby announcing his hurt feelings by moaning through the open passenger window. Both animals made Bett chuckle. She was exhausted but didn't care. The whole morning had been a joy of work she loved to do. She switched on the radio to an oldie about a song that made the whole world sing, and belted out the harmony in a husky alto. Baby joined in.

It was a joy just to get out of the house. In the two weeks since her mother had been with them, Bett hadn't often been able to escape. The ceilings were now all washed. Grout sparkled in the bathrooms. Cans of soup were lined up in the cupboard. Everything was put away. Bett couldn't find a thing, but her mother couldn't conceivably take on another project that involved scaling heights, acquiring blisters, or expending great amounts of elbow grease. Luckily, Bett had intervened in most such instances. Since even the closet corners now reeked of disinfectant, Bett had felt reasonably safe in leaving the house that morning. Her mother couldn't possibly find anything more strenuous to do than make a peach pie.

"Mom?" she called absently as she let herself in the front door. Still humming, she took off her boots and made her way to the downstairs bathroom to wash her hands, using the same hand cleaner Zach did, the only product that really worked on grease. Unlike Zach, though, she finished the job with apricot hand cream. Still rubbing it in, she wandered back to the kitchen.

"Mom?"

With a slight frown, Bett poured herself a cup of coffee and took a sip as she wandered back out of the kitchen toward her desk. Setting the cup down, she curled up with one leg under her and reached for the week's receipts for orders of peaches and plums. Three receipts into the pile, Bett reached for the coffee cup, then set it down again. *"Mom?"*

The prickling up her spine felt like a mother bird's instinct of danger to its young. Bett stood up, knowing full well Elizabeth's Lincoln was in the yard. Her mother generally considered fresh air a trial one had to endure in order to go to and from shopping. Hence, the lady was in the house.

And the lady was not answering.

Bett took the stairs two at a time. She peered first into her mother's bedroom, then her own, then the bathroom. The door at the end of the hall was closed, that spare room that was eventually to be the nursery.

Bett opened the door, stopped short, and swallowed a long, deep breath.

Her mother was wearing her pink tennis shoes, aqua pedal pushers, and an orange bandanna. A ladder was perched in the middle of the floor, surrounded by tarps and old sheets. A jumble of rollers and paintbrushes dripped paint. Mint-green paint. Three gallons of it.

"Brittany! How *could* you come in here! I had planned this to be a total surprise!" Elizabeth glared at her daughter in comic dismay, though somewhere in those doe-soft eyes was a bouncing anticipation of Bett's sure response.

Bett, for the moment, couldn't give it. "Mom." She rushed forward as Elizabeth came down the last two steps of the teetery ladder. "What are you *doing?*"

"You can *see* what I'm doing, silly one. Honestly, Brittany, I knew you had this room in mind for a baby sooner or later, and I thought this was one way I could pay you and Zach back. Zach just will *not* take any money from me, and here I am staying in your house, eating your food..." Elizabeth rubbed the knuckles of both hands into the small of her back, a gesture that indicated how physically difficult such a project was for her. "Aren't you pleased?" she asked suddenly, the smile on her face fading as she noted Bett's stillness.

Pleased? If she'd known her mother was using the most rickety ladder on the farm, she would have been developing ulcers. "Mom. I don't *want* you doing anything like this—"

"I know that. What does that have to do with anything? Brittany?" Elizabeth's face rapidly took on an unsure look. "You don't like the color?"

Bett hated the color, but that was neither here nor there. She felt possessive about this room. Her mother could have absolutely anything Bett had, but this room had been a private thing for Bett from the instant she and Zach had made plans for the house. She and Zach were going to do it together, when it was time for the baby. A gentle cream color for the walls, with murals of kittens and racoons and gentle lions, big and bold and soft. *Not* green.

Elizabeth's eyes suddenly filled with tears. "You didn't like it? I felt so sure you'd be thrilled—"

Bett moved forward helplessly. "I am," she assured her mother, and forced a smile as she hugged her. "I am...I was just...overwhelmed for a moment. And angry with you."

"Angry with me?"

"For taking on something like this with your arthritis. Dammit, *look* at you, Mom."

"Don't swear." But unconsciously, Elizabeth had been trying to rotate a swollen wrist. She stopped the instant Bett mentioned her arthritis. "It's nothing."

"It *isn't* nothing. Mom..." Bett stared in despair at the half-painted room. The bright mint green caught the morning light. Some greens did well in sunlight. This one turned putrid. What was she going to do about her mother? In the meantime, she had an orchard to spray that afternoon; Zach had taken on enough jobs in the last two weeks. And she really had to tackle that bookkeeping; the workers had to be paid tomorrow.

"You don't like the color." Elizabeth's lip was quivering.

Bett whirled. "Of course I do."

"You don't."

"I do."

"I was so sure you would love it."

"*Mom. I do!*" Elizabeth was rubbing her sore wrist again, a waif at fifty-four in her orange bandanna and pedal pushers. "Mom, I really do," Bett said softly. "And I'm grateful for the thought, really I am. You're a very special generous lady and I love you for it. But you're not going to paint this room; it's just too much for you."

"Well, you don't have time." Elizabeth tugged down her blouse. "I admit it was a little more of a job than I had originally anticipated, but I'll manage, Brittany. I'll just take it slower—"

"What I'm counting on you to manage is Zach's lunch," Bett intervened swiftly. She tried out an impish smile. "I was looking for an excuse to play hooky this afternoon anyway."

"You always have so much to do . . ."

"Not this afternoon, I don't," Bett lied blithely.

Her mother allowed herself to be gradually bullied downstairs. Then Bett returned alone to the nursery and stared at the green walls for a few moments in silence.

It wasn't that she didn't know exactly why her mother continually upset her—and why she kept letting it happen. Mother and daughter were coming from two different generations, and worse, two different systems of values. Because Bett didn't live her mother's lifestyle, Elizabeth seemed to feel she was being criticized for her own choices. You *must* see that what I've done all my life is important, she continually told Bett ever so unconsciously. A feminine woman, by the standards of Elizabeth's generation, kept a clean house, prepared for babies, and didn't ride tractors.

Two weeks of subtle criticism, though, had depressed Bett. Not because she was unhappy with her own choice of lifestyle, however. It just wasn't a simple thing, two women's different definitions of "woman." She couldn't conceivably argue with her mother when Elizabeth was going through a rough period. And her mother really couldn't see that Bett had anything more important to do than paint a room in ultimate preparation for a baby.

Bett picked up the paintbrush, stared at the strange green color dripping from it, and sighed.

Zach strode through the doorway, his arms crossed over his chest. At the sound of his footsteps, Bett glanced down from her perch on the ladder, regarding her husband's flinty blue eyes with a sick fluttering in her stomach. Surely he realized Elizabeth was responsible for the painting? He knew his wife well enough to realize mint green was not among *her* favorite colors. So why did he look angry?

"Hi there," she tried brightly.

Zach said nothing. He often walked into this empty room at the end of the hall, for no reason, really. This odd feeling would hit him sometimes, and he'd find himself by the window in here . . .

"Zach?"

An odd uneven pulse was beating in his throat. They'd argued about finishing this room or not. They'd argued over the architectural plans for it; they'd argued square footage and the shape of the window. They had agreed to let it stand empty until they were ready to start a family, which had made perfect sense to both of them. At least, he'd believed it made sense to both of them. The pulse in his throat kept throbbing. It seemed very foolish to feel hurt about this; Zach had never considered himself in any way oversensitive. It was just . . . Bett was his whole family. And he could have sworn she'd understood his need to be involved when a baby was made part of that unit.

"You know if you'd waited just a couple more weeks until the harvest was over," he said quietly, "I would have helped you."

"We can do it over," she said swiftly. She realized suddenly that he hadn't even noticed the color. She had to explain, and yet she didn't want to sound as if she were *accusing* Elizabeth. It was bad enough to be harboring uncharitable thoughts about her own mother . . .

"It doesn't matter," Zach turned toward the door. "Be back in for dinner."

He was gone; Bett was still swallowing the huge lump in her throat, trying to find the right words to say.

6

"HOW ABOUT A little game of three-handed bridge?" Elizabeth suggested brightly.

Zach, stretched out on the couch, lifted his eyes from the farming journal in his hand. It was after ten. He'd just finished sixteen hours of work, give or take quick breaks for meals, and if he hadn't needed to catch the latest weather report on the late news, he would already have been sacked out upstairs. "Thanks, but no, Elizabeth," he said evenly.

"Brittany? Of course, we can't play bridge with only two, but these are other card games..."

Bett was already rising from the opposite couch, rapidly swinging her feet to the floor. Her muscles ached from painting. Her head ached as well. In fact, everything ached. Spraying all morning, painting all afternoon, payroll until ten minutes ago . . . She forced herself to a standing position with a miraculously energetic smile for her mother. "I'll play."

"A good game of cards will relax us both," Elizabeth announced.

"Yes." Elizabeth looked as relaxed as a bouncing ball. Bett trailed her into the kitchen, stifling a yawn. "Maybe we could just play for a few minutes, Mom. I'm a little tired."

Elizabeth glanced up from the card drawer with a hurt look. "If you really don't want to play—"

"I do. Really." Particularly if keeping her mother busy meant a few minutes of peace and quiet for Zach. After doing both his own work and half of hers for the past two weeks, Zach was understandably exhausted. Apart from tiredness, though, he wasn't in the best of moods. If Bett hadn't yet managed to claim a moment of privacy with him to explain about painting the room, the least she could do was insure him some peace. At dinner, Elizabeth had chattered on and on.

Bett settled in a kitchen chair while her mother expertly shuffled the cards. "Canasta or poker?" Elizabeth questioned.

"Canasta."

"I think poker. We haven't played that in a long time."

"Poker, then," Bett agreed.

"On the other hand . . ."

They played canasta. After one game, Elizabeth got up to bring them both glasses of lemonade, and peeked into the living room. "Zach's fallen asleep on the couch," she said fondly.

They played a second game, and were halfway through the third when Elizabeth laid down her cards, perched her elbows delicately on the table, and looked at her daughter. "I've been wanting to talk to you, honey."

"Hmm?"

"Don't you think that you two work together just a little . . . too much?"

Bett's eyebrows arched. "What do you mean?"

"Well. You, going off on those tractors. Lifting bushels. Being around that . . . crew of *men*. Sweetheart, look at your nails."

Bett dutifully looked at her nails. All ten were there, clipped very short. Her small hands didn't fare well with physical work, which was why she constantly plied them with hand lotion. They were never going to pass for the hands of a lady of leisure, but she couldn't see any actual deformities.

"See what I mean?" Elizabeth said gently.

"Not exactly."

"Many, many women," Elizabeth said obliquely, "make the terrible mistake of letting themselves go after they've been married a while. Just a little. As if once you've caught the man, you don't have to worry anymore about keeping him."

Bett shuffled her cards back together, scooped up her mother's, and started putting them back in their cardboard box. "I'm almost positive Zach isn't on the verge of divorcing me because of the state of my hands," she said dryly.

"Now, don't get defensive."

"I'm not getting defensive."

"I was married to your father for a long time, you know. We had a good marriage, a very good one. That took work on both sides, Brittany, don't think it didn't. The hunt and chase is very exciting before you're married, but then a man suddenly realizes he doesn't have to chase anymore, once the ring's on her finger. Humdrum sets in. Don't tell me you don't know what I'm talking about, because I've never met a woman yet who hasn't gone through it. The man's just not in as much of a hurry to pursue, so to speak."

Bett cupped her chin in her palm. She'd been through a lot of these lectures with her chin cupped in her palm. For some strange reason, though, she had an odd stricken feeling inside. Humdrum didn't apply to her and Zach. Luck, undoubtedly? Actually, it was Zach. But for the last two weeks, Zach really hadn't seem to mind that their lovemaking had been interrupted every time, nor that their touch-and-tease contacts throughout the day had been curtailed. Bett swallowed suddenly. "What is it you're suggesting?" she asked quietly.

Elizabeth smiled in triumph. "Several things, really. Darling, don't you think Zach could be tired of seeing you in jeans and work clothes every day? And what exactly do you think he feels when he notices grease under your fingernails?"

Bett didn't know. It had never occurred to her before. She'd thought more along the lines of the pleasure of doing work together than the appearance of her hands before they were washed. Dirty fingernails were...rather disgusting. Which was why she was always careful to clean her hands thoroughly and use the apricot hand cream liberally, but she'd never really thought of how often Zach had seen her fresh—or not so fresh—from the fields.

"And you doing rough-and-tumble work. Man's work. Honey, do you think so much has changed over the generations? A man still likes to feel he's bigger and stronger than his woman. All men like to protect, to believe they're taking care of their wives. If you take that away from him, maybe he sees you less as a woman?"

"Mom." Bett took a long, weary breath. The whole conversation was ridiculous, but a most undesirable flicker of doubt was suddenly preying on her already jangled nerves. When they were first married, she'd invariably come home from work in a dress or skirt. Zach had inevitably commented on her legs, the scent she wore. He was so damned impatient half the time that they'd skip dinner, or forget it. He'd always been...impatient. But the last couple of weeks, he hadn't seemed to care at all that they'd been interrupted. Maybe...

Elizabeth pressed her advantage. "You used to wear padded bras to build up your figure. A little makeup, darling. And your hair, if we had it cut and permed—"

Bett's eyebrows shot up in alarm. "I had ten thousand permanents as a child. They never worked."

"Maybe this time—"

"No, Mom."

Elizabeth sighed. "Well, makeup, then. You're going to be thirty in a few years, Brittany; you *must* take care of your skin. You're in the sun all the time, and you don't want to get wrinkles, for heaven's sake..."

Zach, yawning, shoved his hands in the back pockets of his jeans and wandered toward the bright light in the kitchen. The living-room clock said it was past midnight. He had evidently fallen asleep on the couch. Every one of his muscles was a mix of stiff and sleepy, but the murmurs from the kitchen announced that the two women were still up.

He paused in the doorway, blinking hard to adjust to the sudden dazzling illumination. Elizabeth was bending over her daughter, who sat in one of the kitchen chairs, and when she straightened up, he saw the array of tiny vials and bottles on the table, as well as his wife's face. "Better," Elizabeth announced critically.

He blinked again. Bett's sun-golden complexion had turned ivory; the natural coral of her cheeks had turned pink. The shape of her mouth looked different, sort of a Cupid's bow. Her eyes looked faintly Chinese.

He glanced at the kitchen clock to verify that it was indeed after midnight. He stood there for a few seconds more, unnoticed by the two women, feeling a mixture of amusement and irritation. Not that this new look wasn't very interesting, but where was Bett beneath all of it?

The thought echoed in his mind as he silently climbed the stairs. Where *had* his wife gone? Painting rooms in the middle of the harvest season, spending half her day inside, distracted all the time. He'd expected changes when Elizabeth came, but not that his wife would turn into a stranger.

Bett tossed her head, stuck her hands in her pockets, and entered the cavernous darkness of the huge old barn.

The beams stretched up for three stories, and from the top she could hear the low, melodious coos of the homing pigeons greeting her. Pulling open an old wooden door, she entered the shop.

The room was a stark change from the tall beams and mellow character of old barn siding. Zach had added modern lighting and a smooth cement floor to the shop three years before, and neat metal bins stored the spare parts and shop tools that had once been strewn every which way.

The John Deere was parked on the far side of the long room, and Zach was crouched over the engine, a wrench in his grease-stained hand. On a packing crate next to him was a sterling silver tea service. A thermos of coffee stood next to an alternate option of iced tea; next to that was an assortment of homemade cookies, still warm. Bett's eyes traveled over her husband. His jeans were pressed with an impeccable crease these days. His work boots, underneath the day's layer of dirt, had been freshly siliconed. His blue chambray shirt was starched. Well starched.

The incongruous touches of sterling and starch ordinarily would have made Bett chuckle. Zach was being spoiled, Elizabeth-style. But no smile crossed her features, because Zach once upon a time, became extremely uptight if the least fuss were made over him. These days, he hadn't said a word. Obviously, he didn't much mind being spoiled; even enjoyed it, perhaps. Which was exactly what Elizabeth had been preaching to her.

Zach's head swiveled around at the sound of her footsteps. He had the same oddly distant expression in his eyes that she'd seen all too often this past week.

"Caruso just called," she told him. "The truck'll be here any minute."

Zach nodded. "Our last, you realize?"

"Our last," she agreed, with a fleeting, sharing smile. The battle season was almost over. When the harvest was done, it didn't mean an instant end to the work, but it did mean they could pay off their loan with a comfortable sum left over and begin to relax. Her fleeting smile widened irrepressibly, turning joyous. "Hey, Monroe? We're actually making it. You realize that?"

Zach chuckled, tossed down his wrench, and crooked a blackened finger in her direction.

"No, Zach. *No*. Behave—"

"I need a hug." He caught up with her before she could reach the door, stretching both long arms around her shoulders to imprison her, his grease-darkened fingers splayed in midair behind her. Her eyes were very bright blue this morning, full of laughter. He hadn't seen quite that look in her eyes in nearly a month, and he wasn't about to let her go that quickly.

"Listen, Buster. If you get grease on this white sweat shirt, my mother—"

"Will have something to do besides starch my work shirts." His lips closed on hers swiftly, and lingered until Bett's hands slowly crept around his waist to hang on.

He liked the feel of her arms around him, and he liked the feel of her pelvis cradled directly between his thighs. He didn't much like the feel of lip gloss over the smooth natural texture of Bett's own lips. He drew back just a little to look at her. Bett's skin was as soft as a baby's, skin that begged to be touched. The eye makeup did sexy things for her eyes, but he just couldn't understand why she wanted to hide her natural softness under a layer of . . . crud.

"You're staring," Bett murmured.

"Probably."

"You don't like what you see?" The question was teasing, but Bett suddenly looked as vulnerable as a kitten.

"I *always* like what I see." To hell with it. He was hardly going to say the wrong thing and risk hurting her. It was her business, if she wanted to wear a little paint.

He was in the mood to wear Bett. To pull her on, tuck her in close, and button her up inside of him. Quickies seemed to be all they had the time or energy for these last few weeks since Elizabeth had been there. And when they did catch a private moment in bed, his wife was always worrying that her mother would pop her insomniac head through the bedroom door. Bett's willingness to make love was unchanged, but Zach could sense her distraction. He understood just fine... and for three minutes of real privacy with her, he would willingly have auctioned off portions of his soul. Cheap.

"Zach." Bett tried to pull away. "There's a truck due—"

"If you move even an inch, you'll have greasy fingerprints all over your shirt," he murmured.

True. Bett obediently stood still, offering up her most mischievous smile. She pressed closer to him, since that was obviously what he wanted, and then weaved her hips just a little, a motion she'd learned in the single belly-dancing class she'd conned the girls in the dorm into investing in, about a thousand years ago.

Zach sucked in his breath. His chin nudged aside her hair, exposing a spot on her neck for his lips to explore. Come to think of it, he'd always been partial to that vulnerable spot just below her ear. Probably because she inevitably shivered when he kissed her there.

Her arms tightened around him and she raised up on tiptoe, rubbing deliberately against him, teasing the tips of her breasts against his starched shirt. Inside the stiff collar of his work shirt—the so *very* stiff collar—she tested a puppy-soft tongue. Just a little lick. His skin was sun-warmed and faintly salty; she could smell the earth they both worked on and loved. The man-smell was underneath that. That certain musky scent and nakedness were inextricably linked in her mind. She lifted up on tiptoe again, arching against him, her hips suggesting a familiar rhythm.

She could sense more than see Zach's hands lift to hold her, and hesitate. "Do that again," he murmured next to her ear, "and watch how fast you get taken on the floor of the barn."

Her sparkling eyes met his. "You think I'd object?"

"I think your fanny would."

She peered over her shoulder at the subject under discussion. "It doesn't object."

The chuckle rumbled from his throat at the same time that his teeth nipped at the curve of her shoulder. "You just told me twice that Caruso was coming. Now, behave."

"You're not behaving. Why should I?"

"I don't feel like behaving. I feel like . . ."

She got the message. The look in his eyes was X-rated. The next kiss was delicious. Zach kissed dry; she'd never liked wet lips. She liked smooth, warm, dry lips pressed directly on hers, followed by that sudden wet warmth when tongue touched tongue. "You've been in the honey," he murmured, and went down to kiss her again.

When he surfaced for air, Bett was trembling and no longer smiling. It was ridiculous, really, after all this time to still feel the same wild reaction to the touch of him. The shudders didn't actually touch her skin; it was all inside. A weak-kneed feeling that it was better to lie down, that it was really an ideal time to lie down and feel the warm, welcome weight of Zach on top of her. His devilish eyes were communicating the same message.

She drew back an inch. He drew back an inch.

"We could always meet on the floor of the barn about two hours from now," he said vibrantly, releasing her.

She chuckled. "You want help loading the truck?"

"What I want is for you to visit China immediately so that I don't have to be embarrassed when the truck driver gets here."

She glanced down at his pants. "You're blaming me for that?"

"A hundred percent."

"Most unreasonable. All I did was innocently walk in here, and . . . Zach?" As she was about to go out the door, she turned to him, and hesitated suddenly. She hadn't really come out here to tell him about the truck. She'd come out here just to . . . talk to him, but now the words seemed to jumble in her throat. "Everything's . . . all right, isn't it?"

He frowned slightly, cocking his head. "Like what?"

"Like . . . things." Bett hooked her fingertips in her pockets, staring at a spot just past his shoulders. "Look, I know I haven't been pulling my weight since Mom's been here . . ." *Haven't you missed me working next to you? Haven't you needed me next to you?* "And the house, everything's so different. I know you must be bothered by certain changes, and I . . ." Maybe it wasn't driving him crazy to the extent that it was her, but surely he was annoyed by the starched shirts and the salmon? "We've barely had time together." She bit her lip. "And my mother . . ."

Zach was beside her in three long strides, pressing a kiss on her forehead. "Don't be foolish," he said roughly. "None of that matters. I'm not complaining, two bits. Have you heard me say one word?"

"No," she admitted with a little laugh.

The laugh was hollow, not what he was expecting, and Zach frowned as she turned away. He knew she was making a massive effort to keep her mother's mind off Chet; she was doing a terrific job of it. Bett had a priority in her life that for a time had to partially exclude him; he understood that. He'd wanted very much to reassure her . . . but the smile he'd expected to light up her face wasn't there. That instant before she'd turned away, Bett had suddenly looked terribly unhappy. It didn't make sense.

Zach banged three times on Grady's dilapidated screen door, then let himself in, taking the three steps up into the old farm kitchen.

"Who is it?" called Grady's gruff voice.

"Zach."

"Be with you in a minute."

Zach tossed his cap onto the old oak table and dropped into a chair, stretching out his legs. His eyes scanned the room, from the mound of unwashed dishes in the sink to the row of hats piled on the far counter. The place was far from spotless, and very comfortable. A place where a man didn't feel like he'd committed a mortal sin for having dusty work boots.

"What's new?" Grady loped through the doorway, hitching up his trousers as he glanced around for his pipe.

"Nothing."

"Want some coffee?"

"Have you got a beer?"

Grady's bushy eyebrows lifted just a little, but he opened the refrigerator and brought out a can of beer. He set it in front of Zach, who picked it up but left it unopened.

"I've spent the entire lunch hour," Zach remarked, "listening to the story of Mildred Riley's life."

"Who the hell is Mildred Riley?"

"Damned if I know." Zach rolled his eyes in exasperation.

Grady slid into the chair across from him and raised both legs to prop his feet on an empty chair. "You're not having a little trouble, having two women in the same house, are you?" he asked wryly, and peered out the window. "Where's the truck?"

"Hiding behind your barn."

Grady nodded, as if that were a perfectly logical answer. After a minute or two of silence, he rose and got himself a beer, popping the top noisily as he settled back down.

"She's driving me *nuts,*" Zach said finally. "Plastic flowers all over the place. Salmon. Every time I try to start a conversation with Bett, she jumps in. You ever worked up a sweat in a starched shirt?"

Grady smothered a grin. "Can't say I have."

"Don't."

"I won't."

"I walk in and she's got a drink waiting for me, ice-cold. She chases me down when I'm out in the field with home-made cookies and lemonade. She's so damned *nice*."

Grady took a long slug of beer and wiped his mouth with the side of his wrist. "You told Bett how you feel?"

"Of course I haven't told Bett how I feel," Zach said irritably. "Bett's got enough on her plate. A few months ago, Elizabeth couldn't get through a day without crying; Bett's turned that around so fast it makes my head spin to think of it. I'm proud of her." Zach turned the cold can in his hand. "I've backed her up as much as I can, being out of the house so much. Tried hard to let her think none of it's bothering me."

Grady fixed Zach with an even stare. "Seems to me Bett just might be even more upset than you are."

Zach shook his head. "Just the opposite. In fact, for the first time since I can remember, they're actually getting along together."

"You think so?"

"I know so."

Grady shrugged. "Maybe. I didn't get any smile when I drove by the last time. The times I've seen your wife with-out a smile on her face I can count on one hand. As in lately. I think you've got just one too many women in that house."

"Well, there isn't any question that Bett wants her mother there." Zach sighed.

"Actually," Grady said slowly, "I don't much care what she wants. I'm telling you I expect a smile when I ride by your place, and lately I'm just not getting it. Women," he added, "are strange."

Zach gave him a wry look.

"Excepting your Bett. She's not like most. Now, I wouldn't go so far as taking all the trouble of trying to un-derstand *any* of them, but it does seem to me . . ." Grady stood up, hitching up his trousers. "There's nothing more fragile than a peach. You have to handle them real careful or they bruise. And sometimes a bruise starts on the inside."

Zach stood up, sighed, and frowned at the still unopened beer can in his hand as if he'd never seen it before. Setting it down on the table, he stalked toward the door.

"Want another?" Grady asked blandly. "Seeing as how you've taken up drinking in the middle of the day?"

With a faint chuckle, Zach pushed open the screen door and went back out to work.

7

BETT VIEWED THE tiny hole in the truck's radiator with a scowl. Radiator holes were high on the list of last-things-she-needed on that particular afternoon. How had the branch managed to poke all the way up there, anyway?"

"Brittany, what on *earth* are you doing?"

"Just take it easy, Mom." Bett swung back into the driver's seat and leaned over to open the glove compartment. "I promised you we'd have sweet corn for dinner, and we will." Sorting through a mélange of screwdrivers and maps, she finally found an unopened package of gum. Popping three sticks in her mouth, she started chewing vigorously. The gum, naturally, was stale.

Elizabeth regarded the wad in her daughter's cheek with a scandalized expression, and then sighed. An "I have come to the end of my rope and I guess you have, too" sort of sigh. Elizabeth stared out the window, dressed for the corn-picking outing in purple slacks, a ruffled pink blouse, and the ubiquitous pink tennis shoes.

After their earlier excursion into town, Bett had changed into a disreputable pair of jeans with a hole in the thigh, old sneaks, and a red crinkly cotton blouse that was disgracefully faded, and one of her favorites.

She continued to chew.

This morning, her mother, trying to help, had gotten rid of the patch of weeds growing at the corner of the house. Bett's prize herbs, those weeds. Later in the morning, Elizabeth had announced her intention of going into town to buy a carpet for the green room. A white carpet was what she had in mind. White carpeting and Bett's housekeeping formed a combination that was never going to work, nor did Bett want her mother buying anything like that for her. Moreover, a white carpet and children didn't seem to be a good blend—not the way Bett had in mind to raise childen.

The two women had come home from shopping four hours later. Elizabeth was frazzled and visibly upset with her daughter; Bett was keeping a very, very tight rein on her patience.

Finally, the sugar was all out of the gum. Bett popped the wad on her finger, leaped down from the truck again, and leaned over the radiator. The thing was cool, or cool enough. They were within a quarter of a mile of the house. She removed the rag that had temporarily slowed the leak and jammed the gum in its place. The leak stopped. Elizabeth was peering at her from the open window.

"I don't *believe* you just did that."

"Zach'll do the permanent fix when we get home, but this will get us there," Bett promised.

"I never heard of such a thing!"

"Zach will be mad as a hornet," Bett said glumly.

"He should be. Women in my day and age wouldn't have anything to do with that sort of *mechanics*."

Bett sighed, wiping her hand on the rag as she returned to the truck. "Zach will be mad because I found the only straggly branch in the entire orchard to run over and get stuck in there."

Elizabeth looked startled. "He shouldn't be mad about that. It was an accident."

"But this pickup is accident-prone. I think it's losing its will to live," Bett said dryly. "Nasty thing. It *knows* we need it to last one more year before we can replace it."

"There'd hardly be a worry about replacing it if Zach were working in a law office right now—and you could be at home, not working at all. Having children. I keep waiting for both of you to regain your senses."

She just wasn't going to let up, Bett thought wearily. Her mother, to be honest, rarely got into such a relentless mood. Bett knew well that Elizabeth would be perfectly happy right now if a roll of white carpet were sitting up in the spare bedroom, ready to be laid down. It wasn't just her reaction to Bett trying to put her foot down tactfully but firmly. It was coming home from shopping empty-handed. To Elizabeth there was no greater sacrilege.

Bett turned down the dirt road that separated the pond from the garden, absently noting young Billy Oaks's bike shoved up against a tree. There was no sign of the boy, but she knew the pond was his favorite haunt in the summertime and after school. It made her a little nervous. Billy could swim well and had his parents' permission to come here, but she still felt uneasy at the thought of the child alone near the pond.

"I will never understand why you put the garden so far from the house," Elizabeth said as she got out of the truck and straightened the ruffles on her blouse.

"Irrigation, Mom. It was closer to water here. We could just pipe it in from the pond."

"I suppose so." Both of them reached into the back for the bushel baskets Bett had brought, and suddenly, for the first time all day, they were smiling at each other. "There is *nothing* better," Elizabeth admitted, "than the thought of fresh sweet corn dripping with butter."

"Nothing," Bett agreed fervently.

"Your father loved sweet corn," Elizabeth said softly.

Bett gave her mother a hug as they walked along the tall rows of cornstalks. "He and Zach could go through a dozen ears at a sitting, couldn't they?"

"Ruin the entire rest of my dinner, both of them."

A slight breeze ruffled the tops of the cornstalks. Just the faintest smell of fall wafted through the air. The late afternoon sun spread a golden glow on the land, but it lacked the heavy heat of a summer day. Bett lifted her head once, certain she had heard a strange, discordant sound in the peaceful landscape, but she heard nothing more and returned to the task at hand. Ears of corn plopped one after another into the basket. What they couldn't eat for dinner she would freeze.

"Brittany—" Her mother emerged from behind the second row. "Do you think we have enough? I—"

"Do you hear something?" Bett raised her head again. The breeze flowing through the orchards could produce strange whispers at times. But they were not near the orchards now, and she still kept hearing the same faint whimpers.

"Hear what?"

"I don't know." Bett stepped around the basket and out of the cornfield. She stopped, listening again.

"Brittany, there is absolutely nothing there. I swear, you were always the most fanciful child—"

Bett saw Billy suddenly, about a hundred yards away. Just a flash of orange T-shirt and jeans and his towhead, a glimpse of his wiry, thin body clambering up into a tree. Nothing unusual, yet she found herself taking a first step toward him, and then another.

"Where are you going?" Elizabeth demanded.

"I'll be right back, Mom." She took another quick step, then started running. The old apple tree he was climbing had to be a hundred years old and was mostly hollow. Not that Billy wasn't as surefooted as a cat, but some instinct kept whispering to her that something was wrong. The towhead suddenly turned his head and saw her.

"Mrs. Monroe! Hurry!" The faintest glisten of tears in his eyes caught the sun. The child was so upset he could barely talk. "I saw her in the road, a mother raccoon. She'd been hit. I saw her when I was on my bike, and then when I put the pole in the water, I kept hearing them. *Listen!*" he said urgently.

She'd already heard, even if she could barely understand his incoherent speech. She was about to assure him calmly that it was simply too late in the year for newborn wild creatures, but there wasn't much point in that. She could hear the weak mewlings, apparently coming from a high hollow branch. The creatures making those high-pitched whimpers had no interest in nature's usual rules. They were clearly frantic for a mother who wasn't coming back. "Honey, get down," she ordered the boy.

"We *have* to get them!"

"And of course we will," she promised, and squeezed his shoulder reassuringly once he was safely on level ground next to her. Helplessly, she stared up at the trunk and branches, aware that the old tree wouldn't take the weight of a human being. "Billy, Mr. Monroe's mowing in the orchard just by the house. You think you could take your bike and go flag him down for us?"

"Can't we just get the babies ourselves?" Billy asked anxiously.

"We'll try, but I—" She whirled, only to bump into her mother.

"Brittany! Are you completely out of your mind?"

"Mom." Bett sighed. "Look, I'll be right back. I'm going to get the truck." She raced across the field and bolted into the front seat of the pickup, shoved the gear into reverse, crossed her fingers in prayer for the radiator, and slowly backed up to the base of the tree. Then she scrambled out of the cab, vaulted onto the truck bed, and stared upward again. She could just reach the limb, but not into it. The whimpers above sounded desperately weak. There was nothing to see. No way to reach them; the tree, only half alive, wasn't solid enough to climb.

"*Thirteen shots*. That's what you get, thirteen shots in the stomach if a wild animal bites you," Elizabeth warned.

"Now, take it easy, Mom," she said absently. The tiny mewling cries were tearing at her heart. Grabbing a reasonably sturdy branch, she swung up one leg. The bark crumbled beneath her sneaker and suddenly she was swinging free. *Dumb, Bett*. She bit her lip, while her tennis shoe sought a foothold.

"You're going to kill yourself. You're going to *kill* yourself. Raccoons are *rodents*, for heaven's sake— Zach!"

"I got him, Mrs. Monroe! Listen, I'll take care of them, you know. My mom won't mind. If you'll just get them down, I promise you won't have to do anything else. I'll take them home and—"

"Zach, will you talk some sense into her? I swear, I can't. I've never heard of anything so ridiculous—"

Zach was over the side of the truck in one swift leap, his hands roughly snatching at Bett's waist. She let go of the branch, sinking down to the stable truck bed again. Drawing a long, deep breath, she turned to face him, relieved he was there—at least until she saw the cold blue fury in his eyes. "You knew damn well that tree wouldn't hold you," he growled.

His tone stung like betrayal, as if he and her mother had formed an alliance against her. Bett went rigid. "Fine," she said stiffly. "You are absolutely right. So is Mom. You two just go right back home and be *sensible* and *reasonable*—"

"Hold it, two bits." For just an instant, his eyes pinned hers, a sky-blue, hypnotizing hold. *Since when do you jump to conclusions where you and I are concerned?*

"Now, let's just see," he said quietly. He reached up, too, but could only get to the tip of the branch, not inside.

"Lift me onto your shoulders, then," Bett suggested.

Zach shook his head. "Even baby raccoons can bite. And I'd rather put a hand in there myself than let you do it."

"Don't be silly, Zach. What's the difference who gets bit, for heaven's sake?"

"I wouldn't mind," Billy chimed in from the ground.

"Except you," Zach and Bett chorused simultaneously.

"I don't believe this," Elizabeth moaned distractedly. "You two cannot possibly be serious." Her tone was lethal with disapproval. "You will both get down from there this instant and come in to dinner. I've never heard of such a thing! There must be thousands of raccoons in this country, all of them filthy rodents." She turned to Billy. "Young man, you just go on home. Brittany and Zach..."

She sounded as if she were scolding a pair of teenagers. Zach glanced down at her in surprise. "Keep quiet for just a minute, would you, Liz?"

Elizabeth's jaw dropped.

Zach turned back to Bett and rapidly tugged off his shirt. "You will be *careful*." He knotted the shirt ends, making a kind of sling.

She grinned, moved behind him, and shimmied up as far as his waist. Zach's hands reached behind and cupped her buttocks. "Ready?"

"For *heaven's* sake," Elizabeth snapped.

Zach pushed Bett up the rest of the distance to his shoulders. From there she could peer into the hollow limb, and though she could see nothing, there was a sudden silence within. She smiled, humming unconsciously, very low, the same French refrain that won over her bees. The same seductive song that had wooed a fawn into their yard the winter before.

Zach kept a tight grip on her ankles as she leaned forward, her stomach pressing against the back of his head. Slowly, she reached in. Inside the darkened hollow, fur suddenly flew in frantic motion, but she captured a handful of hair and pulled the creature out.

The baby blinked in blind fury at the sun. It was so tiny it fit in the cradle of her palm, all black-rimmed eyes and more tail than body. Clutching it by the nape, Bett wasted only a second to glance at Zach. They exchanged identical smiles before she gently dropped the tiny weak bundle in his makeshift shirt sack.

Another one followed. The third tried to nip her; he got the chorus of the French love song. The fourth . . . for an instant, Bett paused, suspended, with her arm in the hollow of the tree, unable to move. The fourth baby was very soft, very furry . . . and totally cold and still.

"Are there any more?" Billy demanded anxiously from below.

She couldn't seem to answer, any more than she could force her hand away from the tiny creature. So cold . . . Helplessly, she blinked back tears. Zach, being Zach, picked up on her feelings before she had to say a word. "Leave it, babe," he whispered roughly. "Think of the ones with life."

She took a breath, and pulled her arm free from the hollow. A moment later, she had shimmied back down to the truck bed, cradling the sack of squirming bodies to her breast. Zach jumped down from the back of the pickup, and then reached back to help her.

"Now, I *know* you're not going to take them back to the house," Elizabeth said frantically.

Zach supervised the loading of one bike, one boy, two women, and three raccoons into the truck, but his eyes rested thoughtfully on his mother-in-law.

They didn't want food, the little raccoons. They were too exhausted and weak from crying for their mother, and the warm, diluted liquid Bett offered them from an eyedropper tasted nothing like their natural mother's nursing milk.

"So we'll have to force it," Zach said patiently. He was on the kitchen floor next to her, both with their backs resting against the kitchen counter. A bowl of warm milk was on the floor between them. The three babies were swaddled in warm towels, so that only those big ringed eyes and tiny mouths peeked out.

Billy had just left, most reluctantly, after a fairly lengthy phone conversation with his mother. Mrs. Oaks had warmly agreed that Billy could raise the raccoons—but only if he promptly came home to dinner, and only when the Monroes had approved their "release." Zach hadn't done that instantly, to Billy's disappointment. Very gently, he'd explained to the boy that he knew Billy would take good care of them, but not to get up his hopes quite yet. The chances of the wild babies surviving the night simply were not high. If they were sure the creatures would live, they would be happy to give them up to Billy's care. Bett heard Zach's gentle but firm warning—and knew it was only half for the boy. He was looking at her.

Biting her lip, Bett pried open the first reluctant mouth and forced an eyedropper of milk down its throat. The vise closed again; she had to force it a second time. Suddenly, those big eyes blinked open, unseeing in the way of the very young, and one paw with ridiculously huge claws made its way to the top of the towel.

"One more little bit?" Bett coaxed. She started humming again. The little one took one more eyedropper full, then Bett laid the towel-wrapped bundle on the warmth of her lap and picked up the second raccoon.

"Bett," Zach said quietly, "don't count on it too much."

But she *was* counting on it. "If we can keep them alive and eating through the night, they'll be stronger in the morning."

After that they exchanged warm towels for more warm towels and fed them again. And did all of that again. With the baby that seemed weakest, Bett stripped away its towel and held it close to her body, cradling it to her own warmth.

At midnight, they were still in the kitchen. "You know, your mother," Zach mentioned absently, "was really furious with you."

"I know."

"To begin with, she's not a farm woman. Those were honest fears of rabies dancing in her head. A lot of that anger was concern for you."

Bett leaned her head back against the counter. "Zach, I know that."

"I haven't seen one tear out of her since she's been here. She *is* happier, Bett. It's all your doing." Their eyes met. "And she doesn't understand the simplest thing about you, does she?" he asked quietly. "Your feeling for animals, two bits. How could she not know of your feeling for animals?"

Bett didn't know what to say. Her hair brushed her cheek as she bent her head, stroking the soft creatures in her arms. "I care a lot about her, you know. All she's ever wanted is a daughter to share the things that are important to her. And because I have different values, she seems to feel that I'm rejecting hers. So she . . . tries to push her own on me. I really do understand." Bett shook her head absently. "That's just it, you see. I *do* understand. The failure's mine that the closeness isn't there. It always has been."

Zach's jaw hardened. He was seeing the faint violet shadows beneath his wife's eyes that he hadn't noticed before. Failure? Bett was a failure at nothing, beyond occasionally trying to be too many things to too many people. He hesitated, his instinct to quickly reassure her frustrated by a new awareness that Bett must have harbored those feelings for a long time. Quick words weren't appropriate. He wanted to think, and Bett was so tired she could barely sit up. "You go up to bed," he ordered. "I'll stay up with them. Both of us certainly don't need to—"

Her eyes kindled and she stared him down. Zach sighed. "I can just see how tomorrow is going to shape up, after feeding these monsters every two hours all night."

He was going to make a wonderful father, Bett thought lazily. He stood up and added the third raccoon to the bundle cradled to her chest. Ten minutes later, he returned from upstairs with two sleeping bags and their pillows. By then it was time to reheat the milk and wield the eyedroppers again.

An hour later, Bett was snuggled in the sleeping bag, waiting for Zach to finish rinsing the bowl and lie down next to her. "Mom's going to have a stroke when she comes down in the morning," she murmured drowsily.

"And that's the last time you worry about your mother alone," Zach muttered back.

She didn't hear him, her hand slowly stroking one soft, furry head. The three babies were snuggled next to her. "They're going to make it, you know," she told him.

Zach bent to kiss her once, a kiss for his lady who had certainly lived in the country long enough to understand nature's way of life and death. And who never would. Those babies didn't have a chance in hell of survival . . . but they hadn't come across his wife before.

8

"BETT?"

Through a sleepy fog, Bett opened her eyes, reaching automatically for Zach when she saw his face so close to hers.

"No, sweetheart. Up," he whispered.

"Pardon?"

Zach, for some strange reason, was dressed. Jeans, a dark sweat shirt, sneakers. The room was still shrouded in the charcoal fuzziness of predawn; she could barely make out his shaggy brown hair and crooked smile. The same fuzziness muddled her brain as Zach, speaking in whispers, urged her into a robe and slippers, then down the stairs.

At the front door, she was sufficiently awake to at least open her mouth. She was not generally in the habit of walking out the front door in yellow scuffs and her long yellow cotton robe. Zach kissed her just then. Zach kissed her very, very thoroughly.

By the time she surfaced, he was herding her toward the pickup. "The babies—" she protested vaguely.

"Billy took the babies yesterday morning. Don't you remember?"

Sort of. There'd been two nights and a day before the raccoons had changed from reluctant feeders to guzzlers. She couldn't let Billy take them until she'd been sure they would survive.

Last night, though, she'd fallen asleep like a zombie; she only vaguely remembered Zach carrying her upstairs. Now, she regarded her husband with a definitely sensual smile. "You seem to be kidnapping me."

"You bet your bare toes I am." He tucked her in the curve of his shoulder for the drive, aware that he'd woken her from sleep she still needed, but not caring as much as he should.

Something had clicked in his head during the last few days. Elizabeth, so insensitive to Bett's feeling for animals, to something so integral to her daughter's nature. Elizabeth, criticizing Bett so very subtly on half a dozen fronts, always well-intentioned. Elizabeth, forever and with all good intentions, interrupting every moment of closeness between them.

Zach had never intended to complain about the inconveniences Elizabeth's stay was causing for *him*. He not only cared about his mother-in-law, but also accepted Bett's feeling of responsibility for her welfare.

But Liz should never have made the mistake of hassling Bett.

Very complicated issues had been reduced to utter simplicity. As simple as breakfast. Twenty minutes later, he had a small fire going at the edge of the woods by the pond. Bett was staring at him with increasingly bewildered eyes, her soft hair fluffed around her face in a haphazard halo. Wearing yellow inevitably made her appear as fragile as a daisy. Bett was, at times, very fragile. Scrambled eggs were cooking in the iron frying pan; Bett was curled up on the sleeping bag with an old blanket around her shoulders; and dawn's pale, silvery colors were peeking through the woods.

"So." Bett was groping for conversation. "You just

suddenly felt like a picnic at five o'clock in the morning."

Zach spooned eggs onto a paper plate and handed it to her, along with a plastic spoon. Finding plastic forks had proved difficult. "You're going to need this energy," he commented.

"I am?"

His eyes flickered to hers. "When you're all done, I'm going to make love to you so long and so hard you won't know what hit you." He frowned, staring at her. "Hard isn't the right word. I don't want you to misunderstand. I want an hour with you, in complete silence. I want you open for me. I want to bury myself inside your softness."

Her lips formed a startled O that never materialized aloud. A moment ago, they'd been talking about breakfast. She tried to swallow a bite of food, staring at her husband.

Zach looked the same. His brown hair was still the color of chestnuts, all disheveled, his sideburns getting a little long. His skin still had the whole summer's sheen of bronze in it. He was moving casually, his walk lithe and easy, to the pond, where he crouched on his haunches to rinse out the frying pan.

Maybe he hadn't just said all that, she thought fleetingly. Maybe she'd imagined it. Because there was nothing specifically different in the way he looked that could account for an instant, vibrant, delicious tingling in every erotic nerve ending in her body. As he strode back toward her, his eyes seemed to burn into hers with an intense, deliberate flame.

"Eat," he scolded.

Ah, yes. For that energy she was going to need. She took another bite, not the least interested in food. Zach kicked sand on the embers of the fire with the side of his boot, served her the last of the coffee from the thermos, and took the few items involved in his cooking project to the back of the pickup.

The sun was just peeking over the horizon; the smell of dew surrounded them; the pond waters, pearl gray, were like glass. It was a silent world. She watched Zach as he moved about soundlessly, strong and tall and very, very male. Zach smiled so readily. But Zach was not smiling when he looked her way.

"Bett?" His voice was curiously gentle. He took the half-eaten breakfast from her hand. When he scooped her up, yellow blanket and all, she was not surprised. Zach was doing an unforgivably good job of making her feel like a princess, a princess captured by a pirate. Not that she really believed that, but she gave in to the odd, vulnerable feelings inside, that fragile, trembly rush. She nestled her cheek against his chest as he climbed into the cover of the trees.

"Are you angry?" she whispered suddenly.

His lips fleetingly brushed her forehead. "No."

"You are," she said hesitantly.

"Not," he promised, "with you. And you are the only one on my mind at the moment, Bett."

He stopped walking at the crest of the hill, where in spring there was a bed of wood violets and the sun shone down in long, dusty ribbons through the leaves. In early fall, there were no flowers, just the bed of green like a spongy cushion beneath the blanket as he laid her down. She could smell the fresh dampness of morning, the promise of a sultry Indian summer day that hadn't yet arrived. A golden leaf fluttered down here and there in the stillness. The shade was dark and private.

A cool flush touched her skin as Zach knelt beside her, his fingers threading through her hair as he drew her face close, close enough to lower his lips to hers. "You've been keeping secrets from me," he murmured. "I don't like that, two bits. I don't like that at all."

"What secrets?"

His lips swept over hers again, denying her question, his tongue probing between her parted lips, stirring a crazy flurry of emotions. His mouth left hers at the very instant she'd become addicted. He trailed kisses along her profile, so fragile and light she might have imagined them. His fingers were just as gentle untying the sash of her robe, parting the lapels, slipping inside. "When you're unhappy," he murmured, "I want to know about it. Some problems are solvable and some aren't, sweet. I don't give a damn. I want to know."

"Zach, I don't have the least idea what you're ta—"

His blue eyes blazed into hers. "After all this time, if you really think there's something you can't tell me, Bett, you've got a long lesson coming to you."

"But I never—"

Zach was too intent on engraining the lesson to explain. Her robe was in the way. It had to go. He could feel the shiver vibrate through her body when it was gone. She wore some kind of nylon nightgown that crinkled in his fingers as he swept it up and off, baring her sweet ivory flesh to the morning coolness. She needed warming. He had no intention of letting her catch cold.

He reveled the feel of her bare skin against his sweat shirt and jeans, the tease of clothes between them. His hands swept up and down her flesh, searing in warmth wherever he touched, creating fire with the friction of his hands that were never still. "Don't you ever hold out on me," he murmured. "You don't wear a mask, not around me. You put on coverings for the rest of the world, but not for me."

"Zach—"

"I want you like hell," he whispered. "Open, Bett. All of you."

His lips trailed down her body until his teeth could gently pull at the taut pink centers of her breasts. Her hands were fluttering aimlessly at her sides, but already her body was flushing with warmth, exactly what he wanted. Part of her so obviously wanted to talk, to understand where he was coming from; and yet her pulse was already racing. Zach, too, was communicating on the two levels, but he had no problem defining his priorities. He carried her hand to the growing hardness in his jeans and held it there.

Her breath locked in her lungs for a moment, and then her palm rubbed, over and over, that warm hardness encased in denim. His desire was clear. His need for her was just as clear. If she wanted to talk, that wasn't solely for the purpose of hearing words said out loud. One could start communication in other ways; Zach had taught her that a long time ago. And her response was from the heart, as primal as his, her instincts just as strong.

Her lips were suddenly hot and wild, molding themselves against his. Her fingers fumbled for the zipper of his jeans. Why on earth did he have so many clothes on? Her heart kept beating harder, terribly uneven. Was he actually doubting how much she loved him; was that what his enigmatic anger was about? How could he be such a fool?

Zach pushed her hand away. Once his jeans were gone, he knew he wouldn't last long. His patience was forced, but he was determined to try. His palm took a long, lazy path, between and around Bett's breasts, over the satin flesh of her abdomen, finally slipping between her thighs. Her whole body arched against the shelf of his palms, and a silver mist of wanting filled his head, his blood, his body. Bett's lips were suddenly moist and sweet and warm, seeking his, demanding his. His tongue invaded the hollow of her mouth.

She was on fire. It wasn't enough. *"Let* me," she whispered furiously.

Her fingers pushed up his sweat shirt. He let her strip the soft fabric over his head; he let her fingertips slide over his smoothly muscled chest; she loved to do that. Her hands trailed up, curled around his neck, got lost in his hair. He turned and shifted both of them. With her weight on top of him, he spread his legs, pinning her, loving the imprint of her tiny, taut nipples on his bare chest, loving the ache in his loins as he pressed against her abdomen. Her hair swept down, all in a tangle, strands of sun-touched silk that tickled his cheek as her lips sought his again. Dawn had turned into day. Sunlight filtered down, catching in her hair. Her eyes were never more blue than when she was blind with loving, caught up in the sweetest of senses. She thought herself such a seductress.

She so very much was. He slowed the pace she didn't want slowed, but with a terrible effort. He had to bat her fingers away from his zipper again. He turned so that he was next to her and half on top, and then shifted his body downward. His tongue teased her breasts—one, then the other. His palm was work-roughened; he knew that. He kneaded the small ivory orbs, then apologized with the velvet wet of his tongue. He counted her ribs, one by one.

They were all there. He shifted up again, his knee bent, riding the space between her warm thighs. Way back, before they were married, before Bett had slept with him, he could remember well how he had desperately tried to coax her into bed. Rubbing, just so. A jeaned thigh, like now, until her body moved against his, desperately trying to sate itself.

"What are you trying to do to me?" Bett whispered huskily.

The answer was so very easy. To remind her of exactly how it had been with them at the beginning. Remind her . . . but not with words. He could still remember her murmuring unhappily that she couldn't just . . . sleep with him. They barely knew each other. She'd made love before; heart wounds hurt. So they did, but Bett had some terrible misconceptions about herself and loving. That she was safe as long as he kept his jeans on. That it was important to be polite in bed. That it was not quite right that she had this wild, sweet, wanton side; that one

kept one's private fears and feelings to oneself. Out of
fear of losing her, he'd kept his clothes on for a time.
Not hers. Rapidly he'd turned around what she thought
she could keep secret from him. They would keep no
secrets from each other, not of the kind that counted.
Sex was the medium; loving was the message.

Loving was still the message. His lips seared a very
gentle, tender path down her throat, her breasts, her
navel. Soon, the crinkle of soft hair tickled his lips; her
hips tensed violently. He held them still with his hands.
Very still. Like a sweet little whip, his tongue lashed
out, a very gentle intruder.

Silver rain flooded through Bett. Her whole body convulsed, and her fingers clenched in his hair. "Come *up*
here," she said furiously.

Her husband was obviously trying to drive her mad.
The morning sunlight was all around her, bathing her
flesh, a warm weight on her eyes. She closed her eyes,
aching inside. Her body felt like the hot, steady pulse of
a summer rain. She was naked, and so close to the earth
that her flesh felt part of it. Her heart was beating with
a terrible thunder, but around her there was only sun-
shine. Sun and the peace of morning and shade and
silence. Her breath, coming in harsh gasps, appalled her.

"Zach!"

Far too slowly, his lips trailed upward again. Her
hands fumbled for his jeans, racing down the zipper. Her
palms slid around and inside his jeans, curling over his
flat male buttocks, pushing down the denim fabric that
had separated them for far too long.

He had to stand to get his jeans off. Abandoned for
those few seconds, she found herself staring at him, at
his maleness, than at the look in his eyes as he came
back down to her. His eyes were blue-silver with the
first velvet thrust, blue-soft with the tenderness of loving,
silver-sharp with a man's drive to possess. So full he
filled her, so unbelievably full.

"Burn for me, Bett," he whispered. "Hurt with it. All of you."

She tossed her head, wild with fever. All around her was the smell of dew, the smell of Zach, the smell of morning. She surged beneath him, exploding with need. The fierce rhythm of love rushed through her like a wanton silver river.

A stream of sunlight stole through the treetops in celebration of day, at the same time a different sunlight burst inside of her.

"We have," Zach murmured, "a problem."

Bett shook her head drowsily. "*You* may have a problem. *I* have no problems of any kind." She curled her arms around his waist, snuggling closer to his bare, warm flesh. It seemed like a wonderful idea to stay just as they were. At least for the next hundred hours.

"You can be a disgracefully wanton woman, two bits." He nuzzled at the delectable hollow in her shoulder.

"Thank you."

"Insatiable."

"Yes."

"Uninhibited."

She opened one sleepy eye. "Where are all these compliments leading?"

"You *look* like such an angel. Blond hair, blue eyes." Zach shook his head in teasing puzzlement. "I'll tell you, though, you'd never cut the chaste life playing a harp."

She chuckled, lazily sitting up. At a motion from him, she raised her hands in the air. He slipped her nightgown on her, then her robe. Finally, Zach stood up to tug on his jeans.

"So. What are we going to do about your mother?"

The question seemed to come out of the blue. Bett, leaning over to fold up the blanket, shot her husband a startled glance.

"Kick her out when she's doing so well? Obviously

not. Have her continually lay stress on you? That's not going to keep happening, either. So let's talk choices, Bett."

He swung an arm around her shoulders as they strolled back down the path toward the pond. Bett wanted to answer him, but she couldn't get any words out. So Zach was aware of how unhappy she'd been—she'd done her best to hide it from him. She'd done her best to pretend even to herself that it didn't matter. Regardless, she saw no choices. Her mother had been lonely and unhappy and grieving alone; Elizabeth was happy with them. If Bett found the continual pressure wearing, the old game of trying to please both her mother and herself impossible, she didn't see that she had any choice.

Zach pushed aside a low-hanging branch so they could pass. "Well, talkative one?"

"Zach, I didn't think you were . . . bothered," Bett said quietly.

"How on earth could I be bothered? A cold drink's waiting for me even before I want it, slippers laid out, a woman to ask my opinion on everything as if I were an oracle. You think I don't like being spoiled?"

A small smile played on her lips. "You like the starched work shirts, do you?"

"About as much as I like having to abduct my wife and run off to the woods to make love to her in peace and privacy."

Bett sighed. "It's not as though she knocks on the door every night."

"No. Just often enough that you've got half your attention on worrying every time we make love."

They reached the truck, and both climbed in. The key had been left in the lock, but for the moment Zach didn't turn on the engine. He leaned against the door, bemused for a moment by the sight of his wife in pale yellow, her hair whispering in soft dishevelment around her cheeks. The whole subject caused her distress; he could see it in her eyes, and he had the sudden urge to haul her right back into the woods and make it all go away.

"Zach," Bett said unhappily, "all she wants is to care for and take care of. And there's no one but us to make her feel needed."

"Exactly," he said softly. He straightened in the seat, turned the key, and started the engine. "Number one, two bits, we're about to share the stress. You keep something like that bottled up inside again and I'll have to beat you."

"Like you do so often?"

He cast her a severe look. "Just *once*, you could show a little fear."

"I'm terribly sorry."

"Number two. If you don't mind starting with the total inconsequentials. This isn't a criticism, honey, it's just a question. Is there some reason why, after all this time, you're suddenly wearing makeup?"

Bett sighed. "Mother's afraid I've been 'letting myself go.'"

"You certainly have," Zach agreed fervently. "A *very* few minutes ago, you were one hot little—"

"Zach!"

"What else?" His tone had turned serious, almost angry.

She took a breath. She could have drowned in all the little doubts that had been raised in the last month. *Did* a clean house actually matter to him? It wasn't that she wanted to turn into a hausfrau; she doubted she was capable of it, but his values were involved, too. She'd never questioned him. Maybe he found it more restful to sit at the kitchen table and use silverware and china than their old habit of paper plates on the floor in the living room. Stupid, yes?

"But it's details that make up every day, Zach. I push the toothpaste tube from the middle, leave my shoes where you stumble over them at the door. Maybe—

privately—you were annoyed. The thing is, I never thought to ask you." Maybe working together so closely wore on him from time to time; maybe when he continually saw her ramming around on a tractor in jeans and sweat shirt he saw her as less feminine than he once had—

Between the peach orchard and the plum trees, Zach jammed on the brakes and turned off the engine again. The groove between his brows boded ill. "How the *hell* could you have let her do this to you?"

Bett gnawed on her lip. "Mother? She isn't doing anything to me."

"Four weeks in the house and she's turned my confident, sassy wife into a worrywart. What is this? If I'd wanted a wife obsessed with ring around the collar, I would have married one. I happen to be a big boy with strong vocal cords, two bits, and I'm more than capable of telling you if I'm unhappy with how we've set up our life. I'm not. Now, if *you* are, we'll work on it. If you've really suddenly decided you need the floor under the refrigerator waxed, we'll hire someone to do it. You sure as hell aren't going to devote a second to it. You happen to bloom best in fresh air, and I happen to get a kick out of watching you, tiny as a minute, ramming around inside the cab of a tractor ten times bigger than you are. It makes me feel protective, and proud of you, and good inside to know we're sharing the same goals. Generally, it also makes me want to go up and whip you out of there and take you in the middle of a field, but that's neither here nor there." His frown leveled out, a wicked smile taking its place. "I'm used to that reaction, whenever you're within a two-mile radius."

Bett, for some strange reason, had tears in her eyes. Was he shouting? He reached out and tugged her close, drawing her onto his lap, irritated at the limitations imposed by the steering wheel.

"Have we got that stuff clear now?" he grumbled.

"Yes." Very clear, Bett thought. Zach should shout

at her more often. All the mindless anxieties that had been haunting her had abruptly fled.

"And in the meantime, there's an answer for your mother." Zach shifted her next to him, very close, as he started the truck again. "She likes to take care of people. She is never going to survive well alone. She needs to feel needed. Heaven knows, she's into waiting on a man—"

Bett slapped his thigh. "Don't get *too* used to it."

"She's still relatively young," Zach continued absently. "Not unattractive. She's got this rather crazy side and she talks *continually* and there's that insomnia of hers, but maybe we could keep that kind of thing secret for a while."

"Pardon?" Her husband was talking Greek.

He shot her a mischievous smile. "Are you ready for the campaign?"

"What campaign?" Bett asked bewilderedly.

"We're about to get your mother married off, two bits. It's the only answer."

9

BETT SET DOWN *The Beekeeper's Annual* and glanced outside. The library at Silver Oaks was relatively new, with huge windows looking out on the main street of the town. Their small burg had one of everything—one grocer, one bookstore, one druggist, one department store; the single exception being, naturally, seven agricultural implements dealers. Kalamazoo and even Chicago weren't that far to go for real shopping; but as it was, the community was small and exactly to Bett's liking, a friendly, intimate, know-everyone type of place where it was perfectly safe to walk the streets at night.

Staring absently at the tree-lined street, she thought idly that the *silver* in the town's name was a misnomer. The oaks were turning that smooth, buttery gold they always did in early October. A distracted thought; she seemed to have been distracted for the better part of a week. The thing was, whom did she know in the town who might be a good companion for her mother? Smoothing her navy skirt, she stood up and wandered toward the front of the long, book-lined room. Her skirt—donned especially for the trip to town—was paired with a red nubby sweater with a scooped neck and short sleeves.

Her hair was tied back with a patterned scarf in the same colors.

She felt unusually pretty, and just a little more so when Mr. Hines looked up appreciatively as she paused in front of his desk. "I miss you in the summer," he said warmly. "You and your husband are my best winter customers, you know."

Bett chuckled, leaning on the counter. "I'm playing hooky this afternoon, I'm afraid. Though I did come here with a purpose. Word has it there's a new virus attacking bees in the area, but I'll be darned if I can find anything about it in any of the usual trade journals."

Mr. Hines pushed back his glasses. "Do you have the name of it?"

Bett gave it. "But I don't know anything about it except the rumor. Some disease brought up by a hive from Texas, settled in Ohio, moved into Michigan last spring?"

Mr. Hines's forehead puckered, then smoothed out as he motioned to her to follow him. Bett stuck her hands in the pockets of her skirt, an amused and affectionate smile on her face as she trailed behind. Mr. Hines was a librarian to the core, but she had the feeling that he had secret fantasies of being a private eye. Mysteries were his obsession. Books were his turf, and somewhere in the billions of pages on the shelves there had to be answers for everyone.

"We'll try here, first." He motioned.

She had five magazines in front of her before she could have said boo, and rather than leaving her, Mr. Hines licked his thumb and started flicking through pages with her, pushing his glasses low on the bridge of his nose so he could see better.

Halfway through the second periodical, she found herself staring at him. Theodore Hines was rather short; in the five years she'd known him, he'd never worn anything but a gray suit. The kids loved him, in spite of his dignity. He'd probably help a convicted thief if the thief liked good literature—and didn't use slang.

He had to be nearing sixty; Betty knew he was a bachelor. What would her dad have thought of him? she considered idly. Very thoughtful, very shy, occasionally just a little pompous, but no question; true-blue *nice*.

Mr. Hines turned absently and caught a sudden, radiant smile on Bett's face. "You found what you needed?" he asked, as if thoroughly disappointed that the search had taken so little time.

"I think so—if I could take this out?"

"It's supposed to be a reference for the library." He frowned, and then offered her one of his tiny, very special smiles. "I can't say we usually have a run on beekeeping material. If you could have it back to me in a day or two?"

"No problem." Bett glanced at her watch. It was nearing five o'clock. "Are you working late tonight, Mr. Hines?"

"Not tonight." He moved behind the librarian's desk, searching distractedly for his date stamper. He had never once found it on the first attempt in the whole time Bett had known him. "Tuesdays and Thursdays I stay until nine, but Myra takes Mondays and Wednesdays. Then on Fridays—"

"I wonder," Bett interrupted gently, "if you would like to come to dinner tonight?"

"Pardon?" The librarian blinked.

"All this time Zach and I have known you, you've always been so helpful to us. I can't imagine why I've never asked you before," Bett said smoothly. "We're having lamb with a mint sauce tonight. My mother's staying with us; she makes the most wonderful sponge cake. Wouldn't you like to come?"

Mr. Hines turned a gentle shade of pink, clearly flustered. "I . . . I don't know. I have no way . . . you see, I walk to work. It never occurred to me—"

"I could drive you out and Zach will bring you back. That's no problem. You probably don't like lamb, though," Bett said sadly.

"I do. I do. I've always liked lamb," Mr. Hines said nervously. "I never meant to imply I didn't like lamb—"

"You don't like sponge cake with marshmallow frosting?"

"I do. Or I suppose I do. Honestly, it isn't that. I just..."

Mr. Hines just didn't like to make decisions quickly. Another customer approached; he stamped three books with the wrong date and then did them over, glancing up twice at Bett. Honest—I have nothing painful in mind, her eyes told him affectionately.

"I'll be right back," she promised as two more people came up with their books. There was a pay phone in the women's rest room; she dialed quickly. "Mom, do we have enough for one extra for dinner?" Not that she needed to call. Her mother was a big fan of leftovers. Bett thought wryly that she could have brought an impromptu army to dinner and there still would have been food left over.

"Of course. Who is it?" her mother asked.

"Theodore," Bett answered. "Theodore Hines. The librarian in town; he's a wonderful old friend of ours."

"Well, fine. Theodore—you call him Ted?"

Bett tapped the phone with the tip of her nail. "Um. Actually. we'd better stick with Theodore. Be home in a little bit, Mom."

When Bett very gently herded Mr. Hines out of the pickup twenty minutes later, he was still flustered and apologizing for nothing that Bett could figure out, clearly bewildered at being offered a home-cooked dinner. He nearly balked again when he saw Sniper sitting on the seat; Bett resisted the urge to pat his fanny up into the truck before he could get away. He kept his hands folded meticulously in his lap four inches from the cat as she pulled out of the parking lot and headed for home.

"You're absolutely positive this is going to be no bother?"

"Absolutely positive. My mother's name is Elizabeth," she mentioned, and rapidly turned to other subjects. Getting Theodore to relax was all uphill work. Shakespearean sonnets helped, and so did a discussion on medieval music. By that time, the librarian was doing all the discussing, since Bett knew absolutely nothing about the subject, but she'd moved from Mr. Hines to Theodore. A massive breakthrough.

And just in time. They were edging over the last hill before the driveway that led to the house. The sun was just squinting over the horizon in a blaze of orchid and fuchsia hues that for no reason at all made Bett think of making love with Zach.

Zach, as it happened, was pulling into the drive just ahead of her. She frowned absently, noting the outline of a head in the passenger seat of his truck. The last thing she needed at the moment was another visitor just before dinner. Red Hornack stepped out of the vehicle, laughing heartily at something Zach had said, as Bett turned onto the gravel and parked next to them.

Red owned the local feed store. He was a big, blustery, good-humored man with a fluff of red-gray hair on top of his head. He had half a dozen grown children, and had lost his wife a few years back. Bett and Zach knew him vaguely, having stopped in from time to time; he carried rabbit food and salt licks and wild bird seed, the kind of thing Bett couldn't buy for her wild creatures in the grocery store.

Mr. Hines stiffened the moment he saw Red. Bett patted his hand reassuringly. "You know Red Hornack?" she asked lightly, and frantically tried to catch Zach's eye as she bounced out of the truck.

"Come in, come in," she urged the librarian.

"Little Bett!" Red boomed, and zeroed in for a rib-crunching hug.

As soon as she'd recovered, she grabbed Theodore's arm and dragged him toward the door, beaming radiantly at Red. "We haven't seen you in an age—"

"Well, I'll tell you now, I just never expected an invite to dinner this night. Always thought the world of you two kids, always did. Miss my own; they're strung out all over the country these days . . ."

Ah, yes. Inside the door, she took Theodore's suit coat and Red's faded denim jacket. Both men suddenly looked equally ill at ease, glancing around. Bett had only a moment to glare furiously at Zach before she took their arms and led her little lambs in toward the slaughter. "Mom?" she called out brightly.

Elizabeth peered out of the kitchen, her jaw dropping only slightly at the Mutt-and-Jeff duo. Her hostess's smile instantly replaced a look of pure shock. She marched forward when her hand stretched out, a pink flush of shyness on her cheeks matching the ruffled powder-pink shirtwaist with its bright green sash. "I'm so glad to meet Bett and Zach's friends. You're . . . Theodore." She had no trouble choosing the right hand to shake. "And you must be Red." Her hand was pumped a mile a minute. Elizabeth glanced bewilderedly at her daughter. "Dinner will be ready in just about ten minutes, if that's all right with everyone?"

"I'll get drinks." Bett noted that Zach seemed to be finding his open-throated shirt tight at the neck. Very strange. Red wanted a beer, from the can was fine; Mr. Hines preferred a light cream sherry.

The Monroe household stocked neither. Zach managed to come up with the last of the previous year's honey wine while Bett discussed the forecast and seated their guests in the living room. Elizabeth had defected to the kitchen. After five minutes, Bett excused herself—

just for one short minute—to powder her nose.

The downstairs bathroom was already occupied. Zach had his hands on his hips, a disgusted expression on his face, as he pushed the door closed with his foot. "You could at least have called home and *told* me you were bringing someone home tonight."

"Exactly like you called me?"

"Bett, it just sort of happened..."

"So did Mr. Hines just sort of happen," Bett said glumly. She leaned back against one wall; Zach leaned against the other. "But of all people. *Red?*" she moaned. "Honestly, Zach, what were you thinking of? Red is so...lusty."

"*Lusty?*" Zach's mouth twitched. "Two bits, he's got a paid-for business, a host of grandkids running in and out, a house that needs caring for, and financial security."

Bett looked up at the ceiling. "He gives Mom one of those bear hugs and she'll take off for the closet."

"You think your choice is better? Hines might work up to a kiss after a five-year engagement."

"He's a very nice man," Bett said huffily.

"He's as boring as limp lettuce."

A gentle knock interrupted them. Bett swiftly opened the door. Elizabeth blinked, startled to find the two of them in the bathroom together. "I was just coming to help you with dinner," Bett announced brightly.

Dinner just didn't go as anticipated. Theodore sliced his lamb into tiny pieces. Red wolfed his down. Elizabeth sat at one end of the table and steadily kept serving food that just as steadily kept disappearing. The two bachelors had clearly never eaten in their lives before. Theodore, in spite of all his priceless manners, was silently working on his third helping. Bett stared helplessly at Zach. No one was talking. What was this? Everyone was just ...eating.

She pinched Zach's thigh beneath the table. His fork

clattered to his plate. "How's business going, Red?"

"Jes' fine, jes' fine. More of them peas, please, Miss Elizabeth . . ."

"Certainly." Elizabeth smiled.

They listened for a minute and a half to a discourse on the price of chicken feed before the conversation died again. Bett let her fingers wander up Zach's thigh beneath the table. Half a dozen peas jumped from his fork back to the plate. "Extra busy at the library, Mr.—Theodore?"

The librarian looked up. "There's been a rush on Chaucer," he announced happily. "Three English classes at the high school got it assigned at the same time. I had to limit them to a seven-day check-out schedule—"

Chaucer didn't go over very well. Bett seemed to be the only one listening as Elizabeth served sponge cake. As she swallowed her second bite, politely looking at Theodore Hines, Bett was terrified that she was going to yawn. Her left hand strayed to Zach's lap again.

"More cake, Zach?" Elizabeth asked. "Anyone else?"

No-thank-you's chorused around the table.

"Well, I'll just do the dishes, then," Elizabeth announced.

Bett jumped up. "I'll do them. Zach will keep me company. Would you serve coffee to Red and Theodore in the living room, Mom?"

The exodus didn't take long. Bett stacked the dirty plates and carried them to the sink, casting a critical eye at Zach, who was still sitting by his lonesome at the kitchen table. There was definitely a wicked hint of sapphire in his eyes. "Have you taken a look at your left hand recently?" he asked.

"No. Why?" She lifted up her palm.

"It should be blushing from all that . . . activity at the table."

"It is," she announced, and added sadly, "Zach, this isn't going at all well."

"Give them a few minutes." He rose from the table to help her with the dishes. They took as long as they could. When neither could find a single excuse to remain in the kitchen, they both walked just to the door and paused to peer delicately around the corner.

Red was slouched on the sofa, his stomach protruding; he was red-faced and yawning from his huge dinner. Theodore sat next to him, primly erect, his hands fidgeting in his lap. Elizabeth was sitting in the chair across from them, crocheting an afghan. No one was talking.

Zach glanced at Bett. "A bomb might get that group moving, but I doubt it," he whispered.

"We shouldn't have fed them. They both look ready to go to sleep." Bett sighed. "Mom would have considered it a compliment if they *did* fall asleep after one of her dinners."

Zach left to drive the potential beaux home at nine. Shortly after that, Elizabeth declared she was tired, and picked up a book to take to her room. "I think it's a healthy thing that you two have such a wide variety of friends, Bett."

"Yes." Bett climbed the stairs behind her mother and gave her an affectionate hug at the top. "I'm sorry to have landed you with an extra two for dinner."

"You're joking. You know I love that. You have as many people over as you want, anytime," Elizabeth assured her.

Bett took a bath, donned nothing afterward, and climbed smooth-skinned under the sheet to wait for Zach. She heard the truck roll in around ten and then listened to the assorted, muted sounds from below—Zach getting a drink of water, switching off the lights, swearing softly at Sniper who evidently was sitting in the middle of the stairway.

When he saw that the bedroom light was off, Zach entered very silently, closing the door behind him. Moonlight shone in on the comforter, on the soft mound of Bett's figure. She was exhausted; he wasn't surprised. His mischievous moves under the dinner table were still making him smile; it had made a difference, their talk. Not that she couldn't exhibit more sass than sense on occasion, but Bett had always been a toucher—a caress, a kiss, a hug, all of which had been missing whenever her mother had been in the same room. He felt a warm tug of love for his lady, who had just needed a little reminder that they stayed together through thick and thin. These days were a little thin with Elizabeth around, but they were coping. He pulled off his jeans and shirt, then the rest of his clothes, and very carefully made his way to the bed in the darkness, not wanting to wake her.

The sheets were cold. Gradually, his body heat began to transfer to the percale. He moved instinctively to his side, one arm reaching to drape around Bett and drag her into the spoon of his chest and bent knee.

She turned at just that instant to face him, sliding her leg between his, arching her small breasts against him, snuggling provocatively. "You're tired," she whispered.

The hell he was. An amused smile crossed his face as he reached for her. Those hot little button nipples pressing against his ribs roused about a dozen reactions, none of them exhaustion. Her thighs were smoother than silk, but much, much warmer. "You want to go to sleep, do you?" he whispered.

"Yes."

"You don't want to talk."

"I *do* want to talk," she corrected sleepily, her palm sliding down the muscle of his thigh. "Just not at this exact minute."

"You're too tired."

"We both need sleep," Bett agreed in a low, throaty whisper.

He really had to do something to control those teasing impulses of hers. She arched back when his lips found the column of her throat. He cradled her closer yet, his palms splayed on her bottom. Her skin was warm and pliant, fragrant like the night, as provocative as the darkness. A sweet little tremor shook her body when his hand smoothed down the length of her.

The light knock on the door made him grit his teeth. "Brittany?" Elizabeth whispered.

Zach clamped a hand on Bett's mouth. She was too busy swallowing to answer, anyway. "She's asleep, Liz. Need something?"

"Oh, of course not, Zach. I certainly didn't mean to disturb you. Brittany and I have rather gotten used to sharing a cup of tea when she can't sleep," Elizabeth whispered. "I'm terribly sorry."

"It's all right."

She hesitated. "You don't know where she keeps the tea?"

The tea was in the same cupboard it always was. In the kitchen, with all the lights turned on again, Elizabeth beamed at Zach, at the same time sending him apologetic signals with her eyes. "You didn't have to get up, you know; but I have to admit I rarely have the chance to talk to just you."

His dark robe belted firmly around him, Zach smothered an irritated yawn. Bett was all through with interrupted nights. And when the moment presented itself, Elizabeth was about to get a very tactful lecture on privacy. He forced a smile as he settled in the kitchen chair across from his mother-in-law.

"I've been wanting to talk to you alone for some time, anyway," Elizabeth admitted shyly. Her color was suddenly high, matching her bright pink robe with the ruffles at the neck. "Zach, I feel I can talk to you. I always have. Most sons-in-law . . . I just don't think I would have had that feeling."

Zach lifted his eyebrows, the first puff of wind knocked out of his sails. "If you have some problem, Liz . . ."

"Not exactly a problem. It's just—oh, I just feel Chet should have handled this. You know, you and Bett have been married for some time."

"Yes."

Elizabeth dunked her tea bag, then delicately dropped it in the saucer and lifted the cup to her lips. "I don't know how to say this," she admitted with a shy little laugh. "My daughter... I love my Brittany so very much, Zach. She's not..."

Zach waited, not having the least idea how to help her because he didn't have the least idea what she was talking about.

"In the beginning of a marriage," Elizabeth said slowly, "a young couple is so very much in love. But then later, 'in love' changes to loving; it's a very different thing, a much more important thing." Elizabeth pleated her robe four times, and then took another sip of tea. "Sometimes, it takes work, loving. The thing is, Brittany is rather shy, Zach. Hardly a woman of the world. She never has been. One would like to be sure she is happy."

Elizabeth leveled a soft, brown-eyed, puppy stare at him that Zach understood very well was supposed to be meaningful. He floundered. "You mean the farm—"

"No," Elizabeth said swiftly, and lowered her eyes. "Chet would have handled this so much better," she announced.

Zach had the sneaking suspicion that Chet wouldn't have initiated this conversation in the first place. His eyes strayed helplessly to the clock. The witching hour was almost at hand.

"You're rather male," Elizabeth said nervously.

He blinked.

"And in the beginning of a marriage—well, that's one thing. It's later that counts. The years of building. And Brittany's terribly gentle by nature; that just doesn't go away. A man doesn't usually feel... he has to be patient anymore, after a time. Actually, though it's the patience that counts long after the honeymoon. Love isn't just measured in..." Elizabeth paused, taking another gulp of tea, her face poppy red. "Chet would have handled this much, much better."

Zach hadn't missed the theme of the conversation this time, but handling it was something else. Elizabeth was wringing her hands together in her lap, her soft eyes resting on his, communicating how difficult it was for her to discuss the subject. He wished he felt more exasperation. As it was, he felt a swift stir of compassion, and total weariness at the realization that it wasn't likely they were going to discuss privacy when his mother-in-law wanted to talk about sex. "Look," he said gently. "If you're worried about whether Bett and I are happy in bed—"

Elizabeth's eyebrows shot up in alarm. "I wasn't trying to get that personal," she said stiffly. "Honestly, Zach. If you think I would really pry—"

Zach's hand covered hers. "I don't necessarily think we need to mention this conversation to Bett."

"Lord, no," Elizabeth agreed nervously.

"Bett isn't unhappy, Liz."

Elizabeth's poppy color shaded down to pale pink.

"And she certainly is shy. Terribly shy," he said gravely, and added, "she's a good girl."

The phrase sparked a smile. "I—that's just the thing. I always *knew* that. My Brittany is the kind of woman a man wants to marry, not just—"

"She certainly isn't *that*," Zach agreed, praying silently that not an ounce of emotion showed on his face. "Do you think you can sleep now?"

"Yes. I've been worried about this for so long. I wish that Chet could have had this little chat with you..."

Zach stood up; so did Elizabeth. "Everything okay now?" he questioned gently.

Elizabeth heaved an enormous sigh. "Fine," she agreed. "I just knew I could talk to you, Zach. I think we can both go to sleep now."

Ten minutes later, he was cuddled against his delectably hot-blooded little wife, his disgustingly male instincts appropriately subdued when she murmured in her sleep, sensually curving her limbs around him. He knew damn well what Bett was dreaming about. The same thing he was about to.

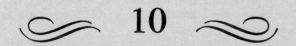

10

FROM A DISTANCE, Zach watched Bett at the hives. The morning sun was bright and warm, even though the leaves in the orchard had already turned gold and brown; it was a glorious fall day. Bett wore a red flannel shirt tucked into her jeans and the crazy straw hat that she'd rigged up with netting that dropped to her shoulders.

She was humming, a husky, low love song. As she slid a tray from the farthest hive, a hundred bees whirled up and around her, and Zach unconsciously shuddered. She *wouldn't* wear gloves, said she just couldn't work with them.

She transferred the tray of honey to the bed of the pickup, where others already rested. He made an instinctive move forward to help her—and stopped himself. Zach was as familiar with the intricacies of raising bees as Bett was; he was also violently allergic to the formic acid in beestings.

Bending over, she accomplished the last stage of the morning's project—transferring brood combs to the new hive in an effort to balance the overabundant population of the insects. It was a sticky, awkward business. Bett whipped off the straw hat in obvious exasperation at its hindrance, and appreciatively Zach shuddered again. Somewhere between five hundred and a thousand honeybees clouded around her.

Finally finished, she very gently brushed them off her shirt and jeans, then walked toward the truck where he waited, the sun glowing on her face.

"You have that look on your face again," she teased.

"It drives me crazy, watching you. If I had to choose between handling those bees and a vat of boiling oil, you know what I'd choose."

"The vat." Bett chuckled, and tucked her fingers into his belt as they ambled toward the truck. "You'd feel differently if you were female. In the meantime, you realize we've got at least two hundred pounds of honey to do something or other with this afternoon."

"I can see that. What I *don't* see is what being male has to do with not loving your bees."

"It's a lady's world, obviously. The queen gets warmed, cooled, entertained, and fed the equivalent of honey steaks, all at her whim. Who'd want to be a boy bee? The drones get kicked out of the hive in winter to starve; they never get to do anything interesting in the summer." Bett swung into the passenger seat, pulling the door shut, and regarded her husband demurely. "The boys are only good for one thing."

"And how you love that line."

"Actually, he must be pretty darn good, considering the queen gets as many as a million eggs out of one . . . um . . . quickie. And I certainly hope *she's* good, since he dies afterwards." Bett propped one foot on the dash, relaxing against the seat. "I've worried for a long time whether he dies happy. Maybe he dies depressed. I mean, he's lived his whole life for that moment, and then what if the queen's frigid?"

"Tough luck," Zach said dryly.

"For the queen, too. What kind of deal is that, to only get to make love once in a lifetime?"

"It wouldn't suit you by a long shot," Zach agreed. His wife sent him a sidelong glance and he chuckled. "Is your mother going to survive our honey harvest this afternoon?"

"I doubt it." There was no reason to expect that life would suddenly take a smooth path after doing hairpin turns all week. Bett had felt worlds better after talking with Zach about her mother, but that didn't change unalterable facts. When Zach wanted her in the woods to help him cut wood for the winter, her mother expected her to go shopping. When her mother had decided to "fall clean" Zach's study, half the receipts for the year had disappeared. And on the first free Sunday afternoon they'd had since summer, Zach had sat down to watch a football game. Elizabeth had spent every football game when Chet was alive chattering next to him. Bett's dad had sort of tuned her out; Zach couldn't.

"Bett, it'll go fine this afternoon," Zach assured her. He added wryly, "We're not doing too well at match-making so far, are we?"

"You'd think my mother would catch on to the odd coincidence that we only have single male friends over fifty."

Zach chucked, but only half in humor. The Monroe household was used to taking it a little easier by mid-October. The grain harvest was still going on; machinery had to be winterized; wood had to be cut for the cold months; but this was still the time of year he had extra time with Bett. Time to rest, time to fool around, time just to steal an afternoon together. And if Elizabeth miraculously found one more project for Bett to do, he would seriously consider strangling her. The instant Bett sat down and relaxed, her mother got nervous. Easy solutions were proving elusive.

The thing about getting Elizabeth married off . . . Zach sighed. No matter how irritated he was with her, he didn't have in mind getting rid of the lady, but getting her involved with other people—something that Elizabeth was curiously shy about initiating on her own.

A handful of neighbors were coming over for their "honey bee" this afternoon. And if a "honey bee" wasn't a good way of forcing people to let down their hair, Zach couldn't imagine what was.

"My Lord," Elizabeth said faintly.

"Now, just relax, Mom. Keep stirring," Bett ordered cheerfully, as she lugged the huge kettle over to the stove. Elizabeth had come downstairs only moments before, dressed "for company" in expensive green linen slacks with a purple and green blouse, having ignored Bett's suggestion that she wear something old. Bett, in jeans and a flannel shirt with the sleeves rolled up, had briskly transformed the kitchen during the half hour her mother had been upstairs.

Honeycombs were stacked on a white sheet on the floor, their sweet smell permeating the entire house. A long table took up half the available floor space, again covered with a freshly washed sheet. On top of that were four five-gallon earthenware crocks and assorted glass jars. The counter next to the refrigerator was covered with cloves, lemon, and cinnamon bark, those spicy smells mingling with the sweet one. Bett was wearing a white sweatband Indian-style across her forehead. And she'd immediately put her mother to work on the opposite counter with two bowls in front of her. One contained oatmeal, the other mud.

"My Lord," Elizabeth said again.

Bett cast a critical eye at the mud mixture. "A little more dirt," she said absently.

Elizabeth, looking more cowed than Bett had ever seen her, added a handful gingerly. "My kitchen," she murmured. "My beautiful, clean kitchen . . ."

"Mother. You are going to have *fun*," Bett insisted. "Really. You just have no idea—"

The front door opened. A chorus of laughter and con-versation floated through from the living room, and in a moment the group descended, packing into every avail-able space and cranny, Zach trailing behind them. He made the introductions. "Liz, this is Mabel Jordan, Su-san Lee, you know Grady, Tom Fellers, Gail, Alice, Aaron, Trudy, Jane—this is Bett's mother, Elizabeth, everyone."

"Zach, you pour," Bett shouted over the ensuing chat-ter.

The glasses were all set out. Zach started filling them from the last crock of the previous year's mead. The women moved about the room, aproned and laughing. They were all neighbors, most of them from nearby farms. The first time Bett had mustered the courage to tentatively suggest a gathering of the local clans, she'd been panic-stricken when they actually swarmed in. Farm women were bossy. It came with the territory. The ones who didn't want honey wine were already fussing through her cupboards looking for instant coffee or tea.

"Less dirt," Mabel, a tall, skinny woman with iron-gray hair, told Elizabeth, peeking over her shoulder. "The consistency has to be just right when you put the honey in it."

"I beg your pardon?" Elizabeth was staring in horror as Grady and Tom Fellers took off their shoes in the doorway, then their socks. Both disappeared. Minutes later, they returned from the downstairs bathroom with bare, and clean, feet.

"Got the brew going?" Grady asked Bett.

"I'm getting it, I'm getting it," Susan Lee told him. "You just set yourself down."

Bett started the burner under the big kettle and mea-sured in a quart of apple juice, two quarts of water, and two pounds of honey. She bumped into Zach, whose arms steadied her as she whipped past him, and knelt to get out a 9 x 13 pan from the bottom cupboard. She

found two, gave her startled mother a quick hug on the
way back up, and then poured the mixture of coeidal
oatmeal and honey into the two pans. In a moment, both
pans were on the floor, and Grady and Tom had planted
their feet in them.

When she glanced up again, she was a little afraid
Elizabeth was going into shock.

"Bett, what do you want me to do?" Alice shouted.

"Hmm. Cut up three cloves, if you would, then the
juice of two lemons for the brew—" Bett popped a large
piece of cinnamon bark into the huge kettle and started
to stir. The liquid was simmering, wafting a tangy fragrance into the air. Suddenly, she stiffened. *"Zach—"*

"I've got the yeast, two bits. Not to worry."

She flashed him a smile. Her mother flashed her a
panicked look that said, *What is going on? You're insane.
They're insane . . .*

"Mud's about ready, Bett," Mabel announced.

"Did you add the honey?"

Dripping a cupful of it across the once-spotless floor,
Bett raced to that counter to add the correct proportion
of honey. "Ready, ladies?"

The other women were sitting down in chairs next to
the tables, scarves tied around their heads to protect their
hair, their faces uplifted and brightened by irrepressible
smiles. Bett glanced around. She'd planned on five. She
was missing one—her mother.

Elizabeth was on her hands and knees, trailing people
with a rag. Firmly, Bett took the rag away and maneuvered her mother gently into a chair beside the others.
"Wouldn't you like a mudpack? Come on, it's fun, Mom."
Her mother didn't answer. Bett started at the head of the
line with her bowlful of mud and honey and stuck her
hands in it. She couldn't help laughing. She was very
sorry her mother wasn't enjoying it, but as she coated
each upturned face with honey mud, she couldn't help
but start chuckling. Grady didn't help matters; he was

slapping his knee as he watched the women. She put some on his nose in passing; he only laughed harder.

"Alice and I are widows, too," Susan Lee told Elizabeth. "Had a terrible time adjusting, both of us. Couldn't sleep. Didn't know what to do with the farm. Never thought things would ever work out again, and Alice had kids still in school, didn't you, Alice?"

When Bett got to the end of the row, Elizabeth's face was—rather stiffly—upturned. Very, very gently, Bett slathered the mixture on her mother's face.

The women kept up a steady stream of chatter, looking vaguely like creatures from a horror movie as the mud-packs slowly dried. Bett had never really understood why Aaron came, except for the fun of the chaos and the drink of apple-cider vinegar and honey she always gave him for his arthritis, but he was keeping up his usual monologue. He dragged a chair over by her mother, who had undoubtedly never considered carrying on a conversation with anyone of the opposite sex while sporting a mudpack on her face. Aaron was an old chemistry teacher turned farmer, white-moustached and tall, and his background showed.

"See, the bees secrete an enzyme that breaks down a chemical something like hydrogen peroxide—you know, like you use on a cut. It's a natural mild antibiotic, honey is, and it's got a water-drawing property—precisely what it does is draw water from the bacterial cells and make them shrivel up and die. See what I mean?"

"I'm not sure," Elizabeth said faintly.

"And not that there's any cure for arthritis, but the vinegar and honey together work pretty well to reduce swelling and take away the pain. It's a soother, inside and outside. Unpasteurized stuff only, we're talking about here. Do you have hay fever?"

"No."

"Well, if you did, honey's a natural antihistamine as well."

"That's very nice," Elizabeth said.

"The girls like it for a face pack."

"I can see that."

"Which is again because of its moisturizing properties . . ."

"Zach, how're we coming?" Bett took a second and a half out for a sigh. She'd been running around like a mad thing. Zach tugged her in front of him, with both arms resting on her shoulders, a very awkward position from which to stir the kettle on the stove. Still, Bett relaxed, cradled back against his chest, inhaling that fantastic sweet and spicy smell rising from the kettle.

"I'll be ready to strain in five or six minutes," he told her, nuzzling his chin on the crown of her head.

For just an instant, she closed her eyes. The next instant she opened them, startled—and delighted—to hear a different tone of laughter in the noisy group behind them. She peeked around Zach. Her mother was laughing. *Her mother was laughing*, her mudpack cracking, the women circling around her.

Bett glanced up at Zach. His blue eyes were doing a tango, waiting to meet hers. Bett was honey from crown to toe. He couldn't offhand see any part of her that wasn't sticky. He had a wayward urge to lick off the shiny spot on her cheek, but controlled himself.

"Why don't you come over for coffee tomorrow, Elizabeth," Susan suggested. "I'll show you how to do that jelly roll. Takes time, I'm warning you, but it isn't all that hard if you watch someone else do it the first time . . ."

Zach didn't exactly know how their honey harvest had mushroomed over the years. Bett had learned beekeeping from a retired neighbor, and had loved it starting with the first spring, but only realized in the fall exactly how much honey there was going to be to jar and sell. Zach had poked a "bee" in Grady's ear, suggesting that one or two women neighbors whose farm season was over might like to help her. "One or two" expanded to a wide group, all bringing their old-time receipes for mudpacks and arthritis cures and remedies for fallen arches. Bett had searched out the old English recipe for mead. The neighborhood theory seemed to be that there was no fun in having half a mess; you might as well go whole hog.

Bett, fool that she was, had encouraged them. Bett had the uncanny ability to gather people of all ages together and bring out their spirit of fun. The thought of a formal dinner party would have panicked her—she'd told Zach a thousand times she just wasn't the type to cope with large groups of people. He let her go on thinking that.

Between the two of them, laughing, they strained the mixture in the kettle, added the yeast, and poured it in the big earthenware crocks to cool. Bett disappeared from his sight then, her blond head popping up here and there during the next two hours. The mudpacks were washed off; the washer was started; one crew tackled the floor and another miraculously produced dishes for dinner. Then there were the dinner leavings to clean up.

Zach watched his wife, a very small locomotive in nonstop action. She was humming most of the time. Quick frowns were replaced by quick smiles, her face vibrantly expressive, her body lithe and free in action, totally feminine.

He loved that lady.

Bett was still humming unconsciously as she said goodbye to the last guest at the door. She loved having this gathering every year, but this year had been special. Her mother had joined in, actually joined in. She hadn't heard Elizabeth laugh so much in well over a year. When Grady had reached out and swatted her mother's rear end in passing, Bett had been thought for a moment that her mom was going to fall over in shock, but she'd recovered. The women had fussed over her like a new hen in the flock. Elizabeth, her pants destroyed, her blouse unrecognizable, her hair flying every which way, had had a very good time.

"The women were so nice," Elizabeth said from the doorway of Zach's study.

Bett glanced up from the book in her hand, smiling. "They are, aren't they, mom?" She was so tired she could barely see straight, but the steady motion of Zach's old rocker had soothed that weariness for an hour now. She set the book down, noting with some surprise that Elizabeth was rubbing her hands as if she were cold.

"That Susan Lee asked me over for coffee tomorrow."

Elizabeth edged into the study, slightly nervous. Bett, perplexed, drew up her jean-clad legs and folded her arms around them. "You're going to go?" she asked lightly.

"Yes." Elizabeth sat on the edge of the couch, primly drew her knees together, and studied the books on the shelf with an absent frown. "That Grady," she said disgustedly. "I have *never* seen a more ill-tempered man. So gruff. I doubt he's had a woman near him in thirty years."

"He is a character," Bett agreed.

"I told him I'd bring him a home-cooked dinner sometime." Elizabeth adjusted the neck band of her orange blouse. "The old coot. I felt sorry for him."

Bett nodded, curiosity and amusement reflected in her clear blue eyes. "That was nice of you."

"He doesn't deserve it," Elizabeth said flatly, and then sighed. "I thought I'd do up a pot roast, some of those small new potatoes, maybe an apple pie—"

Bett smothered a grin. "He'll never recover."

"The thing is..." Elizabeth stood up and started wringing her hands again. "Grady's one thing. Of course I'll take him over a dinner. Brittany, you know I'd do that for anyone. But Grady is not Aaron," she said nervously. "And Aaron. He actually had the nerve to..."

"What?" Bett asked, perplexed.

"Ask me to dinner. Actually like a *date*," Elizabeth said disgustedly. "Can you believe that? At my age? Married for twenty-five years?" She took a book from the shelves, and started leafing through it. "I think I'll read tonight. I'm just too tired to work on my afghans."

Pesticide Management? "Now just sit down a minute, Mom," Bett coaxed.

Elizabeth promptly collapsed in a chair. "It's ridiculous. What would Chet think? Your father would think I encouraged him. I didn't do a thing, Brittany; I can't imagine anything more foolish than people our age—"

"I don't think it's foolish at all," Bett said gently. "Why on earth shouldn't you go out to dinner with him?"

"Because what would your father have thought?" Elizabeth said unhappily.

Bett's words were measured, very soft. "I think Dad would have been delighted to know that someone cared enough about you to ask. And he would have been happy to know you were having a good time. You think he would have liked the thought of you being alone?"

Tears welled in Elizabeth's eyes. "I still miss your father."

"I do, too, Mom." Matching tears welled in Bett's eyes.

Elizabeth stared directly at the bookcase. "They were such good years, Brittany, every one. We didn't always agree, but that never seemed to matter. It's funny, how little that's really a measure of anything. And sometimes... sometimes I get terribly frightened at how very many years I have left. Too many—always to be alone, never to have anyone to *do* for again, to fuss and cook for, to just be with. I wouldn't want anything the same. I would never expect or even want to love anyone the way I loved your father, but I... and then suddenly I

feel so wretchedly disloyal for even considering...
because if you think for any minute I could forget your
father..."

"Mom." Bett pushed herself out of the rocker and
went to lean over her mother, folding her close, smelling
the same faint rosewater scent she could remember from
the time she was a baby. "You wouldn't be disloyal to
go out to dinner with someone else. To see someone
else. You would be pleasing Dad very much. You think
he would want you never to care for someone else just
because he's gone? You just can't think that, because
Dad just wasn't like that. Now, you love to go out to
dinner—"

"Well, I told him no, anyway." Elizabeth rubbed nervously at her eyes. "I still think it's halfway foolish."

"You can call him back. It isn't foolish."

"I've never called a man in my life, and I'm certainly
not about to start now." Elizabeth stood up, and picked
up her book, staring at it blankly. "Besides, I haven't a
thing to wear."

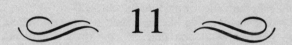

11

"So . . . Brittany." Elizabeth emerged from the closet, holding first one dress and then a second up to her slip-clad body. "What do you think? The blue or the yellow print?"

Holding on to the tag end of a mile of patience, Bett dutifully surveyed the choices. The navy dress was polka-dotted, simple in line, set off by a crisp red belt. The other was a bright splash of orange and yellow and green. "The blue," Bett suggested.

"But the blue would need beads. They're wearing chunky beads this season and I really don't have any to match the dress," Elizabeth explained. "You *really* think the blue?"

"I really think the blue. You don't have to have beads."

Elizabeth turned. "What you *really* think is that I'm worrying too much about going out to this dinner."

The tag end was running out. "It *is* just a din—"

"I think the yellow is much . . . perkier."

"That it is," Bett said crisply.

"With orange shoes."

"Fine, Mom. You'll look just fine." Bett rose from the bed and moved swiftly toward the door. Fresh from the shower, she'd just had time to don an old jump suit before the questions started. She'd been answering the same questions for days. In the meantime, her hair was wet and she was still barefoot; Zach had come in from the woods more than an hour ago and she knew he was starving.

"Then why did you tell me to wear the blue, if you thought the yellow would do just as well?"

Bett sighed. "I do like the blue better, but the yellow is fine. Now, if you don't mind, Mom, I'm going down—"

"I don't like the blue at all."

"Then don't," Bett said ominously, "wear the blue."

Elizabeth steadfastly regarded the expression on her daughter's face, then pulled on a ruffled robe over her slip. "You and I, Brittany, have simply never shared the same taste in clothes. I'll ask Zach."

A very poor idea. Bett opened her mouth to say so, but her mother could occasionally move on winged feet. From down the hall, Bett heard the rapid knock on her bedroom door, quickly followed by a garbled cry. Elizabeth's flushed face reappeared seconds later; she wouldn't meet Bett's eyes. "I forgot," she said flatly, "that Zach sometimes . . . walks around like that after a shower."

Zach, in the next room, was debating whether to leave the door standing wide open or to purchase stock in a dead-bolt company. To close the door was simply without purpose. Closed doors drew Elizabeth like a magnet. Absently, he pulled on a pair of jeans and then a pullover, running a rough brush through his wet hair afterward. After a long run of irritability all week, humor had gradually taken over. An issue of self-preservation.

He'd never really cared if an entire convent saw him naked, but this *was* the week for Elizabeth and doors. Liz always panicked when Bett was on the other side of a closed door—he was beginning to believe she had a hidden device invisibly connected to Bett's thigh that lit up lights when he touched his wife—but this week, she'd picked on Zach. Twice when he was fresh out of the shower, once when he'd been shaving, and once when he had the stupid idea that he could corner Bett for a little kiss and tickle if they were safely behind a door *and* a shower curtain—he doubted that his mother-in-law had recovered from that one yet. Thank God they could still escape to the woods every once in a while for alfresco lovemaking, but the weather would be turning chilly soon...

Elizabeth was remarkable. The farm season was finally winding down. Used to immediately claiming more time with Bett, Zach suddenly found his wife hovered over by a more zealous chaperone than a vestal virgin in early Rome would rate. The lady was rarely shakable. She never slept. Come in for a nice relaxing cup of coffee, and she was full of exhausting chatter. Turn on a football game, and the washing machine went manic. One thirty-second grab at Bett's fanny, and those eyes were all over him. On occasion, Liz hesitantly suggested she might go to town by herself, and they all but pushed her out the door... It was a question of making hay while the sun shone.

In the meantime, if he'd had any idea how much turmoil one simple little dinner date with Aaron was going to cause this household in anxiety and preparation... Zach went down the stairs two at a time, headed for the kitchen, and started haphazardly opening cupboards.

The thought of nutrition made him ill. Broccoli was a very healthy food. Broccoli and salmon loaf went well together; they'd had that combo twice this week. Zach searched the bottom cupboard until he found a can of spaghetti in the very back, one of a few cans Bett had stocked about two years before in case of a winter snow-

in. Not that they'd ever use that kind of thing, she'd told
him. Bett was crazy. He'd lived on the stuff in college.
And the thought of pure starch delighted him.

He opened the can and was pouring the contents into
a pan when the doorbell rang. Absently wiping his hands
on a towel, he strode toward the front door and greeted
Aaron, he hoped without showing in expression or action
that he would have bribed him to take Liz out if the dear
man hadn't thought of the idea himself.

Aaron wasn't really husband potential for Elizabeth
or anyone else; he simply liked conversation and didn't
like to eat alone. An old bachelor at sixty, he was a
gentle man, and provided the ideal means of getting
Elizabeth's feet wet, so to speak. Dressed in simple dark
pants and a corduroy jacket, Aaron smiled easily as he
stopped inside. Zach thought wryly that the poor man
couldn't possibly guess that his arrival had been prefaced
by an entire week of agonizing over hairstyles and new
shoes, deep depressions over the state of Elizabeth's
wardrobe, and searching out the town for matching purses
for every outfit she *might* want to wear.

"Can I get you a drink?" Zach asked, hoping for his
own sake that Aaron would accept.

"No, thanks, Zach. We'll probably have a little wine
at the restaurant. Season go okay for you and Bett?"

"Terrific. Been busy?"

Aaron's schoolteacher background showed. He told
Zach all about his arthritis, his grapes, and the politics
in the community, while Zach moved into the kitchen,
stirring the spaghetti. Finally Bett popped in the door.

"Aaron! How are you?" she said vibrantly.

Zach caught a whiff of Bett's perfume. The nights
were turning cold; she'd slipped into that velour thing
she liked to wear on autumn nights. The wine color gave
her skin a fragile porcelain softness, esepcially in the V
that led up her long throat. Her bare toes peeked out

from the legs of the jump suit; obviously, Bett had dressed in a hurry. Far too much of a hurry—though the style of the outfit was loose and flowing, he could tell from the way she moved that she didn't have a stitch on underneath it. Her hair was wisping all around her face, gold strands only half dried. The smell of her skin drew him, like some hypnotizing—

" . . . All right, Zach?"

He blinked, his spoon still dipped in the spaghetti. Belatedly, he noticed the frantic expression she was conveying with her eyes, the slight, desperate nudge of her head toward the doorway.

"I'll keep Aaron company," Bett prodded him frantically, and then smiled brilliantly for Aaron.

As he left the kitchen, Zach decided quite rationally that he was going to poke little pins into a voodoo doll of Elizabeth if there was even one more tiny problem concerning this evening with Aaron, particularly if she dragged Bett into it.

Elizabeth, as it happened, was standing at the top of the stairs in a blue and white polka-dotted dress, groomed, perfumed, and wringing her hands. "Zach, Brittany is furious with me," she said tearfully. "I'm not going. I just can't go. Please say something to Aaron. I just can't . . ."

Zach took the imaginary pins out of the imaginary doll with a sigh, put his arm around his mother-in-law, and motioned to her to sit down next to him at the top of the stairs. "It's just a dinner," he said soothingly. "But for godsake, Liz, if you really don't want to go, there's no crisis. You don't have to do anything you don't want to do. And if it's going to cause you this much anxiety—"

"The last time I dated anyone—it was Chet, of course—my mother served milk and cookies when he came to the door. For heaven's sake, I don't know how to talk to a man anymore. Not *alone*. It's not that I don't want to go. I even have this terrible feeling Chet would be kicking me for being so stupid."

"Well, I have no intention of kicking you for being so stupid." Absently, he realized that that was a most inappropriate thing to say. "Liz, if you want to go, go. If you don't want to, that's fine, too. It was supposed to be fun for you, that's all, and if the evening is really going to get you this upset—"

"It would be terrible for Aaron if I backed out now, when he's already here," Elizabeth said nervously.

"He'll live through it," Zach assured her. And for all that Elizabeth was a total nuisance who was driving him clear out of his mind, he really didn't want her upset. He was fond of her, felt protective toward her. Any idea of marrying her off was based on caring for her and wanting a good life for her; it had never been a sheerly selfish wish to get her off their hands. On honest days, he occasionally felt like offering sacrifices to the gods that Bett had inherited mostly her father's genes, but that was neither here nor there.

"You think I should go," Elizabeth said distractedly.

"Nope." Zach stood up, his voice firm. "You just got a headache, whatever. I'll take care of Aaron. All Bett and I want is for you to be happy, and for all this trauma—"

Zach's jaw dropped slightly as she stood up and took the step ahead of him, a definite hint of girlish swagger to her hips.

"I've never stood up anyone in my life, and I'm not about to start now," she declared, and turned with a small smile. "Thanks, Zach. I knew I could count on you not to push me." She turned to descend the stairs.

Zach stared after her. Governments would crumble if they tried to use Elizabeth's logic. And for one entire evening, he no longer had to try.

Bett shot him a grateful look when the two came

through the doorway. She didn't know what Zach had done or how, but her mother greeted Aaron all relaxed and smiling, taking his arm as he ushered her out of the house. Bett stared through the window at the porch light shedding a yellow glow on the couple as they walked toward Aaron's car. "Would it be terrible for me to admit I'm perfectly exhausted?" she murmured idly, and turned slightly. "I don't know what you just did, Zach, but I admit I was close to the end of my rope." Her eyebrows rose just a little. Zach was going around the living room turning off lights. "What are you doing?"

"Lock the door, would you?"

"Pardon?"

"Lock the door."

For the first time in the five years they'd lived there, Bett locked the door. "Are we expecting burglars?" she inquired interestedly.

"Is the car gone?"

Bett glanced back at the window. "Yup."

"Want to switch out the yard light for now?"

She switched out the yard light. Night rushed in in an instant; it was equally black inside and out, a dusty black made of billions of tiny charcoal circles all in motion in front of her eyes. "I'll bet there's some point to this," she suggested wryly.

Zach made some muffled answer from the kitchen, where the last hint of faint light suddenly winked off. Bett stood in the silence for an instant, feeling the craziest little chill crawl up her spine. She could see nothing, hear nothing.

In the darkness, a stranger suddenly reached for her, a man she couldn't see but only feel. An inexplicable fear made her stiffen... but in that very same moment her senses registered somehow a very handsome man, even if she couldn't see him in the blackness. He was tall and he smelled like lime and musk and somehow like an autumn wind; his legs were long, the hard muscles pressed against her. As an attacker in the night, Zach was incomparable. His breath mingled with hers just before his mouth closed on hers with unerring skill, the cool taste of peppermint blended with the warmth of his mouth. A delightful crackle of lightning flashed through her bloodstream. Very pure, very potent desire.

"Open," he murmured roughly.

Her lips obediently parted. His tongue thrust inside, firm and soft and deep. His palm cradled the back of her head to insure her closeness, her accessibility. Submissive instincts surged through her. They didn't often play dominant/submissive; they liked things equal, but . . . there was a time and a place.

"Dinner?" she breathed.

A very nice, practical thought, when her hands were already sliding around his back, clutching at his shoulders as her tongue sought further play with his. Her makeshift stranger had brazen hands. In long, slow, intimate sweeps, he was molding her body to his, pressing the velour to her skin. He really was going to have to let her lips go and allow her to breathe, though, she thought.

He did, momentarily. Quick, scattered kisses were pressed on her cheeks, her closed eyes. "You know what that does to me? Knowing you have nothing on underneath that?"

His mouth locked on hers again. This time he put a modicum of space between them, just enough so his knuckles could brush against her breasts as his fingers pushed down the zipper of the jump suit from neck to waist.

This particular jump suit had always fit loosely. His palms slid smoothly inside from her neck to the shoulders, pushing the fabric just ahead of his caress, and with very little effort the thing fell in a soft whoosh to the floor. Black was turning to dark gray as her eyes adjusted. She could make out a shadowed form in front of her pulling a sweater over his head. Her fingertips reached for the irresistible warmth of flesh, of smooth, hard contours. Her touch was possessive, and Zach's breath suddenly roughened next to her throat. Her knees felt oddly double-jointed, something that shouldn't happen to old married women. Zach was just...an intruder for the moment, an intruder with nothing on but a pair of jeans; his smooth-skinned chest was rock-hard, his heart pulsing beneath her palms.

A rush of excitement flowed through her. A callused palm claimed her breast; then he rolled its tip between his thumb and forefinger. Flickers of intense pleasure vibrated through her body. There was such a hush in that darkness. Just the sound of his breathing and hers. The sound of flesh against flesh. The sound of hearts beating out of control. How had the fuse ignited so fast?

"Zach. We're in the front hall," Bett murmured weakly.

Obviously, he didn't care. Beds were very nice and comfortable; he clearly wasn't interested.

Was she supposed to be? She'd almost gotten used to being inhibited, to a distracted feeling of *hurry* before they could be interrupted. There was no one in the house with them. The door was locked. For the first time in far too long, she felt all the promise and richness of privacy.

Silence was golden; the darkness was delicious. Bett flicked open the snap of his jeans. At that instant, however black the room was, she could make out the luminous quality of his eyes. He hadn't uttered a word of complaint in all these long weeks. He hadn't made out in any way that he'd found her any different in bed, that he might be unhappy that she had been less than...totally giving. She saw it now. She saw his patience...and his impatience.

She skimmed off his jeans, her palms sliding the fabric down at the same time that she stroked the hard curve of his legs. When his jeans were off, she was kneeling on the floor; Zach knelt down beside her, arranging a very odd mattress of velour and denim and Orlon sweater. The tile still felt cool and hard beneath that as he urged her down, a cool that her body welcomed. Her senses were that much richer because she couldn't see, but only feel, and taste, and smell, and hear him. That one lost sense heightened all the others.

His palm stroked with sudden softness, stilling the fierce rush of their passion. His fingers threaded through her hair and his soft, liquid eyes sought hers. Bett lowered her lashes and raised up on one elbow, her lips closing first on his mouth, then on his chin, then on his throat. She shifted, slowly, so that her lips could reach the spot right over his heart. Her tongue gently caressed one of his tiny nipples, then the other. They hardened to small points, exactly like her own. Lifting up, she swayed over him, brushing her breasts teasingly against those two hard, dark, tiny points on his chest. Zach's hands clutched responsively at her hips, urging her back down to him. In the darkness, she smiled, gently pushing aside his hands, her head dipping down again.

She could feel wanting in her toes, her thighs, her chest. And power—sheer feminine power. She brushed her hair out of the way, but nevertheless strands stole down to tickle his abdomen as her lips pressed and lightened and smoothed. There were very few places on his body where his skin was soft, not touched by the sun. They belonged, she'd decided a very long time ago, to her. Zach suddenly sucked in a breath and forgot to let it out again.

He reached for her, but she ignored him. Loving was raging inside of her. A man could call it wanting, a woman never. He'd been so patient, so giving, so gentle through this trying time. Zach was human, not superhuman; it had all taken an effort. She wanted to tell him how much she loved him for it, without wasting any time on words.

Her fingertips trembled over his most sensitive flesh, drawing a shudder from him as they stroked through

rough, curling hairs. The lapping of her tongue cooled his overheated flesh. Zach had taught her any number of games to play with her tongue. To tickle, cool, soften, stroke, tease. His six-foot-one-inch frame was a big playground. She raised up and crouched on her knees, her palms slowly caressing the length of his hair-roughened legs. Her mouth was settling in for a new brand of creative kisses she'd just invented when his whole body convulsed.

She sat back, extremely pleased with his reaction. She was even more pleased when he roughly pulled her down next to him. Her body stretched to make full contact with his, sensitive nerve endings igniting like fireworks. "If you were any hotter, you'd be on fire," he murmured.

"You don't want to play anymore?" she whispered.

"A serious business, playing. You just went past Go, two bits. Now you get to collect." His voice changed to a husky whisper as he leaned over her. "Dammit, I've missed you!"

Surely he didn't think he was alone? Her legs wound around him, drawing him in, her hands busy, in long, languid strokes on his shoulders and neck and back, anywhere she could touch. A sweet, sweet wildness kept building in both of them. The front hall of all places; the strange blackness all around them, the cool tile beneath her, the smooth sheen that covered their flesh—all of it induced wanton delights, fresh bursts of trembling desire.

He covered her finally, surging inside of her, filling her. Her whole body arched; his mouth seared on hers; and a rush of hot liquid fire flooded through both of them.

By ten o'clock, the front door was unlocked and the porch light on again. Bett was stretched out next to Zach on the couch, dressed, cuddled, and sleepy. Her eyes were closed. "Don't you think she should be home by now?" Zach asked idly.

Bett opened one eye. "You sound distinctly like an overprotective father with a shotgun across his lap. It isn't as if we both have to wait up for her."

"She's a grown woman. Neither of us has to wait up for her."

Bett smiled, snuggling closer. "I'm too sleepy to move. You've totally worn me out."

Zach brushed back a strand of hair from her forehead, kissed her, and then rearranged her, one of her legs tucked between his, his arm around her waist. Her body was limp, soft, pliant. "I want you again," he murmured.

"You couldn't possibly."

"I do." His palm cradled her hip, drawing her close enough to prove what he said.

"You have the most endless capacity for fooling around of any man I've ever met," she remarked sleepily.

"Ah. The voice of experience talking."

She poked him.

"They could have had a flat tire," he worried.

She chuckled.

The front doorknob clicked open a few minutes later. The two loungers both bolted up to a sitting position, Zach shifting the fit of his jeans, Bett rapidly restoring some kind of order to her hair with her fingers. They were both grinning rather inanely as Elizabeth walked in with a bright smile.

"Well, my goodness, are you two still up?"

"You left at seven. It's twenty minutes after ten," Zach informed her flatly, ignoring the elbow Bett poked in his side.

"Really? I didn't even notice."

Bett gazed at her mother, searching for signs of mental wear and tear, as Elizabeth hung up her raincoat, describing what she had eaten for dinner right down to the rolls. "How I love homemade yeast rolls. But I'll tell you, my breaded veal cutlet is better than theirs. I was telling the waiter, you have to be careful what coating you use..."

Elizabeth disappeared into the kitchen. Bett and Zach exchanged glances, and then Bett struggled to her feet, following her mother. "The thing is, did you have a good time?"

"Of course I had a good time. You know how I love to go out to dinner." Elizabeth frowned as she wandered to the stove and lifted the cover on the stainless-steel pot. "Good Lord. What is this?"

Zach slipped behind Bett. "Spaghetti."

"You cooked it for dinner and then didn't eat it?" Elizabeth asked bewilderedly. "What did you two have for supper, then?"

"We..." Bett floundered.

"There just seemed to be a dozen things we were more hungry for than spaghetti," Zach interjected blandly.

"I should think so." Elizabeth wrinkled her nose at the congealing mess. "I wouldn't like to think the two of you couldn't get by without me as far as making yourselves a decent dinner goes." She glanced at both of them, her eyes suddenly widening with rare perception. "You weren't *worried* about me?" she asked incredulously.

"Of course not," they both assured her.

"For heaven's sake, let's get some sleep, then."

All three of them agreed on that.

12

". . . . AND THE CONTINUOUS use of a specific residual herbicide has traditionally resulted in poor weed control in the orchard..."

The speaker droned on. Zach crossed one ankle over his other knee, and used his thigh as a table for his pad of paper. His pen rushed across the unlined page in flat, bold strokes.

"So in selecting herbicides for orchard weed control, let us first examine diuron, simazine, and terbacil..."

Half an hour later, the farmers were shifting in their chairs. Most of them wanted the information as much as Zach did, but hadn't anticipated paying such a high price to get it—suffering through a monotone delivery so hypnotizing that the audience was blinking continuously in an effort to stay awake.

The meeting finally ended at nine; Zach bolted impatiently from his chair and stalked out of the stale air of the classroom. Pickup doors slammed all around him as he buttoned his alpaca jacket against the stiff November wind. A few other growers stopped to wave or exchange a word or two before he slammed the door of the pickup and started the engine.

At least half of the other farmers were accompanied by their wives, most of whom usually stayed in the back of the room near the coffee machine and shared gossip at these agricultural meetings. Bett usually came, but not to drink coffee. If she'd been there this time he could well imagine her hand waving in the air, the men's affectionate and sometimes amused glances, her very polite demand to know the exact difference in chemical composition between diuron and simazine, what studies had been done on the effects of those chemicals on the environment, and in what conceivable way they might react with other chemicals used in an orchard throughout the year. Last year the agronomist from the local university had not been prepared for such a cross-examination. This year the speaker had occasionally leveled Zach a wary glance, as if waiting to be challenged.

Zach had not been in a challenging mood. Cold air nipped at his cheeks and nose; he turned the dial on for the heater and pulled out of the brightly lit parking lot onto the lonely black strip of road. Snow was in the air. Thanksgiving was a week away, and the last autumn leaves were whirling down in the bitingly cold night. He could have owned the road; no one else was on it.

Fall had always been his favorite time of year. Work wasn't over—work was never really over on a farm—but the pressure was off; there was the satisfaction of a harvest completed and all the luxury of sudden leisure time. When you walked outside, the crisp autumn air burned in your lungs and made you feel alive...

Often in the fall, he and Bett bundled up and walked the farm on a cold night. Just as often, he associated November nights with a hot fire and cider and Bett curled up next to him in silence, her eyes half closed. In the late afternoon, they would gather chestnuts sometimes. And there was the nuisance job of raking leaves—he had half a dozen pictures stored in his head, of Bett making huge efficient piles of crackling leaves; of Bett, laughing, flat on her back, waving her hands back and forth while he patiently explained that one made angels in the snow, not leaves; then of himself on top of her, burying both of them, most methodically...

There had been none of that kind of thing this year. Zach turned down another lonely side road.

This fall had been an exercise in continuous chaos. The household had ridden the merry-go-round of Elizabeth's new social schedule. Popularity had mysteriously sneaked up on his mother-in-law. Zach had dragged home Jim Barker from the bank; Bett had discovered the man who owned the local dress shop, a widower named Fred Case. Then there'd been Horace, Graham, Bob—who made the unfortunate mistake of putting the moves on Liz—Joe Greeley, and the Michaels man. There was someone else; she was often gone at lunch, but he'd forgotten the name. Even the neighbors had become involved in the conspiracy. Everyone knew a widower, a bachelor, a divorced man; Susan Lee had a brother...

Bett and Zach had made lists, checked references, vetted the contenders. Elizabeth did not call the outings dates, because she was too old to date, she said. These were engagements, dully noted on an engagement calendar. Each was a complicated project, involving hairdos, clothes, anxiety, anticipation, lengthy debates over shoes and purses, a pre-hash of worry, a post-hash of exactly what had transpired over the evening.

Elizabeth was under the impression that they always invited people to dinner three or four times a week during the fall. Zach had been coerced into donning a suit and going out at least every other weekend; Liz said four at a table made conversation easier. Company came continuously to the house. No crumb dared fall on a coffee table; one never knew who was going to come by.

Liz didn't seem to be falling for any of the men, but she was certainly happy. Bett was happy because her mother was happy. The chain reaction stopped with Zach.

He'd initiated the matchmaking game, so he said nothing.

Actually, he'd been saying less day by day. And to-night the silence all around him as he drove seemed an outer manifestation of something he felt inside.

A few minutes later, Zach twisted the knob of the front door and let himself into the house. The glare of far too many lights assaulted him first. The rest of the room kind of hit him like a sniper's bullets, one thing after another, as he hung up his coat and, for some strange reason, just stood there.

It was a stranger's room, his living room. A canary cage blocked the entrance. He was fond of animals, but had never taken to caged birds. The bookshelves had been cluttered up with knickknacks. Bett's greenery had plastic flowers sticking out of the pots. A purple, green, and yellow afghan had been thrown over the couch. The furniture had been rearranged—actually, it had happened some time ago, but he just now seemed to notice it. A velvet-cushioned rocker occupied the prime sun spot. Bett's type of clutter—a sweater over a chair, four opened books, the pewter collection of tiny creatures, the spray of dried wild flowers on the coffee table—no longer seemed to exist. His magazines had been banished to the study.

He stared for a moment longer before silently making his way toward the chatter coming from the brightly lit kitchen. He found himself pausing for a moment in that doorway, too, before moving forward. Bett hadn't come with him tonight because she was exhausted to the point of being cranky and wanted nothing more than to wash her hair, soak in a tub, and fall into bed.

Her hair wasn't washed yet. She was still wearing gold cords and his old brown sweater, and she was kneel-ing on the kitchen counter, dragging dishes down from the top shelf and passing them into her mother's waiting hands. Liz popped him her usual bright smile before Bett swiveled her soft eyes in his direction, tossing a "Hi, honey" to him before she impatiently finished a sentence to her mother. He made no reply. But then, Bett wasn't expecting one.

Absently, he opened a cupboard, while tuning in on the newest crisis under discussion. Thanksgiving. Evidently, everything in the cupboard had to be washed before Thanksgiving whether it was to be used or not. The preholiday mania emanated from Liz; Bett was laughing, but her voice was strained.

Zach studied the cupboard's contents. These days the top shelf by the refrigerator held a full supply of alcoholic beverages; they needed those to entertain. After a moment, he decided on neat whiskey, poured a couple shots in a glass, and wandered toward his study.

He closed the door, and a feeling halfway between relief and anger pulsed through him as he slouched down in the old antique office chair behind the desk. The room was peaceful and silent, filled with his books and farming magazines, the oak desk he loved, the burnt-orange carpet that blended in a soothing way with the dark wood paneling. Bett's pewter collection, he noticed suddenly, had been relegated to the top shelf in here. Restlessly, he shoved a booted foot against the desk, swirled the amber liquid in his glass, and after a moment or two, leaned back his head.

He was in much the same position some twenty minutes later.

"Zach?" Bett's head peeked around the corner of the door, her eyes uncertainly seeking the still form of her husband behind the desk. Zach had come in from the meeting with a rare aura around him that spelled *mood*. Her pulse had been beating unevenly ever since, and the cool blue eyes staring back at her didn't help any. "What's wrong?" she said quietly.

"Nothing's wrong. I just wanted a few minutes of peace and quiet."

The words were innocuous enough. It was the slight edge to his tone. Testy, unwelcoming...hostile? Bett forced a smile. "Did your meeting go okay?"

"Fine. Your mother go to bed?"

"Yes." Tight little balls were collecting in every muscle in her body. They had been threatening all day. "Tired?"

"Not really."

He hadn't shut her out like this in a long time. In the next life, Bett decided, she was going to marry a ranting shouter. Zach was unbearably calm in anger. His rare silences sent a tense rush of panic up and down her nerves, anxiety she just didn't know how to allay. "Something *is* wrong," she said hesitantly.

"You've been up three nights in a row," he said flatly. "Just go get some sleep, Bett."

"You'll be up soon?"

"Sooner or later."

She edged back out of the doorway. His tone of voice gave her very little choice. She glanced at the stairs, but found herself wandering toward the kitchen again, dragging her hand through her hair. After spending the last three hours with the silver polish, all her muscles were complaining. Bett felt irritable. Her mother hadn't even thought of the project until after dinner. It wasn't a totally unreasonable idea; they were feeding three extra mouths at Thanksgiving, and Elizabeth always panicked if everything wasn't just so for a holiday. Which was fine. Only now Bett was too darn tired to wash her hair, and when she didn't wash her hair every second day she felt irritable.

And she was about as sleepy as a young baby with the colic. Who on earth cared about hair? Her stomach understood that Zach was angry; it was knotting up in fists. Actually, Zach was very rarely angry. Zach was the easygoing one, the patient half of the pair, the control-over-emotional-upheaval half. When he slipped out of character, it was amazing how fast the whole fabric of their lives unraveled. Absently, Bett gazed around the spotless kitchen, then wandered to the liquor cupboard. She poured herself something or other from a green bottle, took a sip, and grimaced. Firewater, she thought dryly. The stuff did slide nicely down her throat, but it seemed to settle around all the knots in her stomach and not do anything about them. Nor did it miraculously make her sleepy.

There was another sip yet in the glass, which she carried back with her to the study door. Taking a breath, she pushed open the door again. With her chin just slightly uptilted, she very determinedly and in total silence curled unobtrusively in the far corner of the old leather couch behind Zach's desk.

Zach said nothing at her second intrusion. His hair was layered from the wind, thick and brown and warm under the light behind him, but his face could have been carved in marble. He looked strikingly handsome when he was like that. An artist would have seen it: the compelling male, the ice of anger, the pride and control; it was bone and flesh and man and Zach, handsome in a way no other man could be. Only Bett didn't need him quite that good-looking. "It's been building all week, hasn't it?" she said softly.

"There is no crime in wanting a few minutes alone."

"You're angry."

He didn't hesitate. "As hell."

"At . . . me."

"At you."

She set down the glass, thinking of all the times they'd bickered. Zach was darn close to a bastard when he had a cold; she was impossible to live with about the third day into a snow-in. That was bickering. This was something else. If on rare occasions Zach had turned icy be-

fore, that was like the cube versus the berg this time.
And she didn't have the least idea what was wrong.

Zach picked up a pencil from the desk, weighing the
thing in his hands, and then started idly flipping it over,
eraser tip to lead, then lead tip to eraser. "It's way past
time you called it off," he said flatly.

She waited. If that was supposed to mean something,
she most definitely didn't understand what.

"I'm the one who asked your mother here. She always
did strike me as a little off the wall. In a nice way.
Whatever. Maybe I didn't really understand how nerve-
racking she'd be day by day, but I thought I could handle
it." His eyes suddenly met hers, hard and flat. "And over
time, I discovered that I *can* handle it. She drives me
absolutely nuts, but I love her, too. And if I hadn't given
a damn about her, I would have found a way to deal
with her. For your sake," he said quietly. "Only, Bett,
you're undermining both of us, and I'm furious."

She opened her mouth, but he didn't give her a chance
to say anything.

"You're the one who's always had trouble with her,
Bett. I know you as wife and lover, not as daughter.
That whole scene of daughter makes you unhappy, guilty,
unsure—I don't know what you want to call it. Sometime
or other you had to work out those feelings. This seemed
like a good time. She needed you, and you wanted to be
there for her—fine. Because even if every chip was
down, I was there to help. I thought we'd deal with it
together."

"I thought that's what we've *been* doing," Bett said
softly. "I don't understand, Zach. That's exactly what's
been happening—we talked. If you don't think I appreciate what you—"

"To hell with that." Zach lurched out of his chair,
tossed the pencil on the desk, jammed his hands in his
pockets, and leaned back against the bookcase in the
shadows. "I walked into this house tonight and didn't

even recognize the place. It isn't home. It isn't my house. It isn't the place you and I put together anymore. And while Liz may be the one who made the changes, she's made them with *your* consent."

"Now, wait a minute," Bett said defensively. *"You* were the one who asked her here. She could hardly come and stay for any period of time without leaving her things around—"

"If we had a child," Zach interrupted flatly, "I expect the house would be total chaos. Diapers and interrupted love scenes and bottles and crying and dinner at odd hours. I keep thinking about that. Of how I would be bothered by that. But the truth is, two bits, I wouldn't be bothered by it at all."

His head was certainly going faster than hers; she didn't understand the connection. "I don't know what you're—"

"It wouldn't bother me, because chaos doesn't bother me, just like odd dinner hours don't bother me. I can live with an awful lot as long as you're happy. Only you're not happy. Your pewter's been banished to the study and plastic flowers have taken over the living room. I'll laugh if you will—but I haven't seen you laughing. Bett, she isn't sick. She isn't still grieving the way she was. You've had me to back you up, to support you, and you know it. So why the hell are we living in Elizabeth's house?"

Bett uncoiled from the couch, stiff and hurting and suddenly furious at his even tone. She hadn't been prepared for knife wounds this evening. She thought fleetingly that she could be married for a million years and never be prepared for a hurt deliberately delivered by her mate. "Come on. You think that's fair?" she protested. "If our lifestyle's changed, it's because you invited her here. All I've been doing is the best I know how to—"

"You haven't done a damn thing but let it happen," he said flatly. "You know exactly what we value as a couple, what we need as lovers, what the two of us are all about. And it's really as simple as the lock on the bedroom door that doesn't exist—but you bought that lock, didn't you, Bett? It's in the top drawer of the dresser."

She swallowed, folding her arms stiffly across her chest. "I could hardly put it on. I knew just how hurt she'd be if she saw it, how horribly embarrassed at the thought that she'd been interrupting—"

"Right. A lock wasn't the answer. Telling her to handle her own insomnia was. I tried once—and failed. Your mother has a disarming way of being manipulative. But I didn't try again, because the fact is, two bits, it was *your* job. She's your mother. And you're the one who *needs* to deal with her."

He was very still, half in shadow, half in light. Waiting. For what? she thought furiously. "What did you want me to tell her, to stay out because we wanted to make love?"

"Yes."

"Zach, that's ridiculous," Bett hissed.

"No," he said quietly. "It would just be hard. And that isn't the same thing as ridiculous at all. What you and I have built together—you have to stand up for it sometime. Now, if you want me to put it all back in order, I will—so fast it'll make your head spin. This is *not* your mother's house. It's yours. I can do it for you, Bett, but somehow I never thought I'd have to. *Do* the two of us mean something to you?"

Tears burned in her eyes. "Of course we do," she said in a low voice. "How could you even ask that? Zach, if you're demanding that I make her leave—"

He shook his head. "You're not hearing me at all, honey. I don't give a damn if your mother leaves or stays. I'm talking about you and me." He straightened, staring at her. "You'd better think it out," he said flatly. "Soon."

He walked past her, and a moment later she heard the thudding sound of his footsteps on the stairs. She couldn't seem to look away from the blank, empty doorway. The tears dried in her eyes, leaving a salty aftersting. She felt cold. Her fingers curled around her upper arms, rubbing up and down. Zach? So cruel? *You haven't done a thing but let it all happen.* Did he think it had all been so easy on her? How unfair could one man be?

Her head ached, and an odd tremor disturbed the even beat of her heart. Fear. Never in the five years of her marriage had she ever considered that Zach might leave her. He hadn't threatened to leave her now, but it was there, suddenly, the reminder that love wasn't carved in stone and never came with a guarantee.

Déjà vu: She could remember exactly that tremorous heartbeat from when she'd first fallen in love with him. An incredible elation when she was with him, followed seconds later by depression at the thought that she could lose him, followed seconds later by elation again. She'd forgotten about those insane mood swings. Other people in love seemed to exhibit the same psychotic symptoms. But they'd gone away, of course, because once she had the ring on her finger she didn't have to worry quite so much about that love. Did she?

Where had that horrible lump in her throat come from? Darn it, she was exhausted. And confused. She switched off the lights in Zach's study and the lights in the kitchen and headed for the stairs. And then didn't go up. The house suddenly seemed smothering to her. Mindlessly, she grabbed a coat from the front hall closet and let herself out the front door.

Cold wind snatched at her hair and whipped around her cheeks; she gulped it into her lungs. Her legs were in a terrible hurry, walking nowhere. Just down a farm road. A few snowflakes fluttered down, blurring her vision. The uneven earth set obstacles in her path, just small stones and ridges and hollows, but she could barely see in the darkness. She stumbled, yet didn't slow her headlong pace.

It helped, the rush. Anger bubbled up inside of her, shunting aside the unbearable fear. *Zach* had asked Elizabeth here; *she* hadn't. Did he think there'd be no piper to pay, having someone else in the house with them full-time?

For Bett, there'd always been a piper to pay where her mother was concerned. Resentment and love came in the same package. She'd thought that Zach understood. Just as he'd said, for once in their lives she'd wanted to relate successfully to her mother. *Now,* when Elizabeth needed her. And that's all I've been doing, Bett thought furiously. Being good to Mom. Loving her. Caring for her. So where exactly was the crime?

She walked and stumbled, walked and stumbled. Out of nowhere, Zach had turned selfish. Men were the pits. Husbands were the worst. She was not Wonder Woman. She was so damned tired she could barely see straight. Exactly what more was she supposed to do?

She walked through the orchards, over the clover hill, past the woods, and finally stopped at the pond, out of breath. The full moon was partially shrouded by clouds, but that faint silver circle still glistened on the icy waters. The cattails were brown now; frogs and crickets had gone to sleep for the winter. Her fingers were so cold she could barely feel them; she jammed her hands into her pockets.

Zach was clearly being a bastard. Unfair, unreasonable, callous, insensitive. Yet that whisper of fear shivered again through Bett's bloodstream. Fear that came from nowhere. From the wind and the night.

She was so totally different from her mother. She'd tried, so often, to be a Brittany. She'd been trying for almost three months. She'd been miserable most of that time. Just once, she thought fleetingly, she had wanted her mother to say that she understood. The farm, her chosen lifestyle, the zillions of things that made up the person that Bett was. The woman she was.

Winning approval was a game that children played. There must still be some of that child in her, because Bett suddenly saw all too clearly how much she had sacrificed in the last three months, trying to win it. Mothers were such very powerful people. Love wasn't the only thing that made up that blood tie; there was the intrinsic definition of femininity, of everything it meant to be a woman. A mother spelled out her version of that definition first, before anyone else had a chance.

Tears burst from her eyes suddenly, shocking her, choking her. They kept on coming. She'd tried so damn hard. *Damn* Zach. How *dare* he think she hadn't minded the changes in the household, the loss of their privacy? How *could* he accuse her of not valuing the love they had? Couldn't he understand the impossible position she'd found herself in, trying to please her mother, her husband, *and* herself? It was a no-win situation. What on earth did he expect her to do?

What she'd *been* doing was walking a tightrope, trying to live by her mother's standards, trying to appease Zach. *He* was the one who was angry? *She* was the one who'd gotten totally lost in the meantime.

So who let that happen, Bett-Brittany? nagged a most unwelcome voice inside of her. Zach? Your mother? Or you?

The night was frigidly cold. She could not remember ever feeling a wind quite like this one, so unforgiving, so fierce and icy and eerily silent.

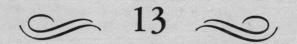

13

Thanksgiving dawned with four inches of crystal-white snow on the ground. At six in the morning, dressed in a long flannel robe, Bett awkwardly pulled the twenty-pound turkey from the refrigerator. The unwieldy bird was certainly more than big enough to feed six. Two weeks before, she and Zach had mentioned to Elizabeth that they always took in lonely strays from the neighborhood on the holiday. That they'd found three unattached men in the age bracket of forty-five to sixty was purely accidental, they'd let Elizabeth believe. But then, two weeks ago, Bett and Zach had been confederates in the gentle conspiracy of finding someone for her mother to love.

Who could have guessed they'd risk losing their own love in the process?

Humming "The Battle Hymn of the Republic," Bett burrowed into the back of the pantry for the huge roasting pan she only used twice a year. For five long days, up until now, she'd been humming funeral dirges instead. For five very stupid days, she'd let anger hum between herself and her husband, a silent song. Two of those days she'd still been furiously angry with Zach. Two more days had been wasted being furiously angry with herself. The one productive day out of the five was yesterday, when with far too painful clarity Bett had tried to put her emotional house in order.

That was done, and battle hymns were now appropriate. It seemed she had a few bridges to mend, none of them small ones. Both careful and immediate mending was called for, and that was not going to be easy, when this Thanksgiving had already been set up as yet another day revolving around her mother. Which was *not*, Bett was finally beginning to understand, her mother's fault, but her own. The last thing she and Zach needed was yet another day interrupted by strangers, which was why she was humming. Humor was armor against fear—fear that her husband was out of both patience and compassion—and Bett had a great deal to put right and *now*, chaotic day or no.

With a cup of steaming coffee on one side and the turkey on the other, she started slicing tiny slips of mushrooms and celery for the dressing. She'd measured a cupful of each when she heard the quiet footstep in the doorway. Zach.

"Morning," she said brightly, suddenly so busy she could barely think. Where exactly was it that she kept the mugs, the coffee, the spoons . . . a freshly brewed cup was set in front of him almost before he'd slid into the chair.

"Morning," he echoed back.

Her nervous system registered a little chill emanating from him, a little startled stare at her exuberance, and about five miles of distance.

"Want some breakfast?"

"Just coffee. You're up early."

When one intended to rebuild an entire life in a day, one could hardly sleep late. "Yes." He wasn't encouraging any more conversation. She took a deep breath and then turned her back, searching for a skillet. He was getting scrambled eggs and ham. He loved scrambled eggs and ham. Whether he wanted them or not was irrelevant.

She stole a few surreptitious glances at him. She loved the look of his hair all tousled from sleep, the softness of his mouth framed in a morning beard, the sleepy-lazy blue of his eyes before he really awakened and took on the world. He'd managed to be out of the house a great deal these last few days. Early to rise, late to bed, and around as little as possible. It was up to her to break the silence; she knew that. Only they'd never had an argument like this one before, where they'd actually hurt each other very badly, where something had broken down that they'd both assumed had a lifetime warranty.

Had her heart picked up a murmur during the last five days? It just wouldn't beat evenly. What if she said the wrong thing now? So she said nothing, but browned the ham, whipped up the eggs, then hurried to the opposite counter to finish chopping. She reminded herself to melt some butter in the microwave to toss in with the bread crumbs. If the dressing didn't get packed in the turkey, the turkey wouldn't get cooked, the people wouldn't get fed, and she couldn't kick them all out to talk to Zach. She could feel his eyes on her back, and her mind reeled through a practice run of what she wanted to tell him. So much, so very much, and it was all lumped in her throat.

The eggs started bubbling. Bolting back to the stove, she stirred like mad, and heard the unwelcome sound of water running upstairs. Her mother was up. This wasn't the time to try to talk to Zach anyway, yet she couldn't possibly keep on another minute with that horrible lump in her throat. She flipped off the stove burner, slid his breakfast onto a plate, nervously rubbed her hands on her robe, heard the ping of the microwave timer, poured melted butter into the bread crumbs, told herself to *stop all this racing,* and set the fork and knife and bowl down in front of him, perching on the edge of the opposite chair at the same time.

"Look, Zach," she started unhappily.

"Happy Thanksgiving, you two," Elizabeth chirped brightly from the doorway, and bent to give first her daughter and then her son-in-law a peck on the cheek.

Bett lurched back up, her total frustration masked by an innocuous smile. "Sleep well, Mom?"

"Wonderfully. Better than I have in weeks—at least until I looked out the window and saw the snow. I just hate winter, the thought of driving on icy roads. Now, that's one beautiful turkey," she complimented her daughter.

"Yes," Bett said distractedly.

"You should have woken me. You know I would have—"

"Bett." Zach's low voice somehow reverberated within her amid her mother's bright chatter.

"—helped you with the stuffing. We'll have to get the turkey in awfully early if we're going to have it done by three. I thought I'd wear the lavender print, though—"

She heard him. That was just it—how often *hadn't* she heard him in the last few months of frantically following her mother's conversations? Her eyes locked on his face, and she was startled to glimpse the first natural smile she'd seen on his lips in days. She savored a fervent hope of a thaw in the frigid barrier between them for several seconds before she noticed where his hands were motioning.

Elizabeth, unfortunately, had already turned around. "What on earth is Zach doing with the stuffing?"

"Nothing," Bett said stiffly. She whisked the bowl back to the counter and put his plate of cooling eggs on the table in front of him. Brilliant, Bett, she thought morosely, thoroughly demoralized. Maybe she should offer up a prayer that at least she hadn't stuffed the turkey with scrambled eggs.

Her spirits rallied when she saw her mother zeroing in on the turkey. "Nothing doing," Bett said firmly. "Mom, you've been cooking for us for weeks. Now, I know that's been your choice, but it's my turn. Just sit down, and I'll make you some breakfast."

"Brittany, I am hardly going to leave you with all this to do by yourself."

"Sure you are." Bett steered a cup of coffee toward her mother's hand. "Think of it as a vacation day. A 'feet up' relaxer."

"Well..."

Elizabeth was persuaded to sit down, bribed with a slice of peach coffee cake. Bett whirled back to her turkey, her mind rushing through the morning's organizing of recipes and cooking. The menu included her whole-grain zucchini bread, honey-glazed carrots, the sinfully rich Coeur à la crème—roughly translated as Cream of the Heart. She didn't dare look at Zach. He was undoubtedly going to see this morning as yet another instance of Bett slaving in the kitchen over her mother's choices. They were *hers,* and it mattered so very much that he understand that. Chop, chop, chop. Even her cleaver was picking up determination.

Her mother suddenly was hovering over her shoulder, the coffee cake obviously having exhausted its appeal. "I've always loved Thanksgiving," Elizabeth mentioned idly.

"Me, too."

"I could do that for you."

"I'd rather do it myself, Mom." Bett poured the last cup of chopped ingredients into the huge bowl and started stirring.

"You're going to add raisins, aren't you? Your father always liked raisins in the stuffing."

"Actually, no," Bett said weakly.

There was a moment of silence for this bit of heresy. Bett spared a longing glance for her still full, now cold, cup of coffee on the counter. She should have managed at least one full quota of caffeine before anyone was up. Why was hindsight so cheap? And why did this whole scene feel like Custer's Last Stand?

"I think," Elizabeth said thoughtfully, "you should add raisins. I always do." Bett felt her mother shift restlessly behind her. "Actually, Brittany, you should go up and get dressed. I could finish the stuffing for you, and then later you wouldn't have to be in such a hurry..."

"That's okay, Mom. There's plenty of time."

"You're not going to add raisins." Elizabeth pursed her lips. "That's up to you, of course. It never occurred to me that you didn't like them. You never said anything, all the years you lived at home. And every single Thanksgiving..."

The pause was Bett's cue to give in. Not that there would be an argument if she didn't. Just very gentle needling, perhaps a sentimental blur of tears in her mother's eyes for scorned traditions, and the unconscious message that Bett was doing something wrong. Like a sponge, Bett had always soaked up guilt. Obviously, there was something terribly wrong with her for wanting to make stuffing without raisins.

Raisins?

Bett suddenly felt sick. She'd planned a tactful confrontation with her mom, but, truthfully, over something far more heroic than dried fruit.

"Each to her own taste," she said mildly, thinking that perhaps it *was* easier to start with the little things. In your house, your way, darling. In my house, mine. The first bridge was just saying it aloud.

She glanced over her shoulder after a moment or two. Her mother was staring at her with an odd expression as Bett stuffed the raisinless mixture into the bird.

"I have a story to tell you," Bett continued cheerfully. "The very first year we were married, I cooked Thanksgiving turkey for Zach. I got out two cookbooks and memorized the instructions and told Zach I didn't want any help. I must have basted the thing every two minutes; it was a miracle it ever cooked, but that's neither here nor there. You never let me in the kitchen as a kid, Mom, more's the pity. I didn't realize the turkey was...um...hollow inside. Much less than there was anything inside the holes..."

Her mother's mouth was slowly starting to curve into a smile; so was Bett's. "I called Zach in to carve when it was done, *so* proud of myself. He said he'd first get the stuffing out for me, so out came the heart and gizzard and neck and all, still in the paper bag. *Very* well cooked they were. So was the paper bag. What on *earth* is that? I asked him..."

Elizabeth started laughing. So did Bett. Bridge two, she thought wryly. Mom, I would like to announce that you have a daughter capable of doing some very foolish things. I don't want your damn approval. I just want to share.

Her mother's eyes were sparkling with laughter. "Why didn't you tell me that before? Sweetheart, did *I* ever tell *you* the story of when I was first married..."

No, she'd never told Bett the story. Bett had always been under the impression that her mother never made mistakes in the kitchen, that Elizabeth had been born with the ruthless efficiency to manage a faultless house. Bett's eyes flickered to the table. Zach had left the kitchen. She wished he were there. She wanted him to see that she *had* heard him, that the small bridges were being mended.

Her mother suddenly reached over and hugged her, and Bett hugged back. "Brittany, we're going to have a wonderful day!" Elizabeth announced.

Bett was suddenly not quite so unhappy that Zach had

disappeared. All the bridges didn't have to do with Zach. Her relationship with her mother was separate in itself.

Her heart was in both corners, but there was no question, not for an instant, where her priorities were.

She loved her mother; Zach was her life.

"That was an absolutely wonderful dinner!" Wynn Hawthorne pushed himself back from the table, patted his stomach, his white head shaking in appreciation.

Wynn was a retired insurance man, with all the gregarious conversation that went with his trade. Bob Lake owned a local processing plant; he seemed a quiet, austere man, and he'd lost his wife three years ago. Garth Hawkins, the bearded giant, had four generations of farming behind him.

Heaven only knew why Bett had thought they would blend at the table over a Thanksgiving feast. They did have one thing in common—being lonely strays—but only a manic optimist would have believed that was enough. Not that talk hadn't flowed easily enough, but Elizabeth was sitting silently on the other side of the table, rarely drawn into the conversation. She seemed to lack any interest in any of them . . . actually, to an almost unusual degree. Once Elizabeth got over her shyness, she'd always been naturally curious about people.

Awkwardly, Bett stood up. "Dessert, everyone?" Awkwardly, she started to clear the plates. "Awkwardly" summed up the entire afternoon, and she felt ridiculously close to tears. She'd been swamped with chores in the kitchen all morning; there hadn't been an instant to talk with Zach. Twice he'd walked in—once the blender had been roaring, and the second time Billy Oaks had popped in the door. His mother obviously had kicked him out so she could prepare her own Thanksgiving feast in relative peace; in the meantime, he'd brought the thriving raccoons over to show Bett. Of course, they'd gotten loose in the kitchen.

She hadn't seen Zach again until she was letting their company in the front door. Her dress was dark red, a velvet jersey. It had stitching under the bodice that almost made her look busty, a gentle flow to the skirt, feminine medieval sleeves, a soft V to the neck. She could not conceivably look better. She'd violently threatened her hair to stay in its pins; tiny strands curled around her cheeks and the nape of her neck; mascara and shadow highlighted every seductive potential she had in her eyes; and she'd applied perfume lightly in every wicked hollow.

Zach hadn't noticed.

She looked perfectly beautiful, and he hadn't noticed. The three men had arrived on top of each other; she should have guessed why. Halftime. She'd managed to set the turkey on the table between football games, as she expected half the women in the nation were doing. That part was fine, or at least sort of fine.

She'd just had different expectations of the entire feast. It was *her* menu, *her* organization of the dinner and the house and hostessing the guests; she wanted Zach to see that. She'd had hopes that the guests would keep her mother entertained, and she would have a little one-on-one time with Zach; Zach was going to have an easy, relaxed meal and Bett was going to confidently, brilliantly, handle the peripherals and when the day was finally over they would talk.

Only the plan had crumbled. Wynn kept throwing an arm around her shoulders; she hated men who touched so carelessly. Garth was pompous and just never stopped talking, and Bob was a military enthusiast who conjured up world wars for enjoyment.

Before they'd been invited to dinner, her guests had certainly given very different impressions. As she scraped the plates in the kitchen, Bett decided glumly that all men showed their true colors when put in front of a football game. The next time she vetted someone for her mother, it was going to be at a fourth and goal in front of a TV set. In the meantime, Zach's relaxed dinner had gone by the wayside. Zach was *not* a military enthusiast, hated pompous people, and his repeated icy stares at Wynn could have refrozen the turkey.

Elizabeth carried in another round of empty dessert plates, her cheeks flaming. "Did you hear what that Garth said?" she hissed.

Bett nodded. Garth liked simple talk—all four-letter words. Who would have expected that of Susan Lee's brother-in-law's cousin? "Now, I know he wouldn't deliberately offend you, Mom. It's just his way of talking."

"We should have salted his turkey with detergent," Elizabeth announced blandly.

A wisp of a smile appeared on Bett's face at the idea, but it quickly faded.

"What's wrong with your hair?" her mother asked curiously.

Bett's fingers raced up to her hairpins. The ones that were all sort of hanging in midair. "Nothing." She pulled them out, one by one. Who cared? The day was destroyed. Her grand visions of handling the holiday had gone the way of dust. It was *her* house; she was in control; they were about to go back to living the way she and Zach liked to live; and her mother was going to be well loved but ousted—gently—from the director's chair. This was not a movie set.

Fine.

Only seeing was believing, and how could Zach possibly believe she had such monumental changes in mind after the hours that had just passed? She *had* to talk to him.

"They've settled into another football game," Elizabeth remarked.

Of course.

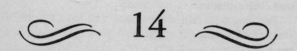

14

RESTLESSLY, BETT PICKED up the vials of perfume on her dressing table. There were only three. Shalimar was a scent that generally made her feel wanton and seductive; she usually paired it with the black see-through blouse she never wore out in public. Charlie smelled like summer, like daytime and sunlight and freedom.

L'Air du Temps was her favorite. She lifted the tiny crystal bottle and sprayed a hint on her throat, then impatiently set the vial down again, wrapping her arms across her chest. The whole bedroom was beginning to reek of it, primarily because that was the fourth time she'd reached for it. Dutch courage just wasn't forthcoming.

Zach had left to go for a walk more than an hour ago and still hadn't returned. Elizabeth was in bed; their guests had been gone for two hours now. At ten, with the kitchen in some sort of reasonable order, Bett had gone upstairs. Now, twenty minutes later, she was still pacing the room, still dressed in the dark-red velvet jersey, every nerve keyed up to an unbearably high pitch. Zach, would you *please* come home, her heart kept crying. She chewed on a fingernail, staring again at the empty doorway.

* * *

Soundlessly, Zach turned the knob of the back door and let himself in. His cheeks were icy and his hands stiff with cold as he took off his coat. Outside, it was still snowing; distractedly, he ran a hand through his still-damp hair before glancing at the stairs. Downstairs it was cool and silent . . . and empty.

The long walk had chased away half the cobwebs of a most tedious day. The other half hadn't been banished nearly as easily. Zach was angry. He'd been angry for the better part of a week.

His eyes had followed Bett nearly all day. The expression on her face, half humorous, half terribly anxious, when she'd served him a fork and knife and bowl of dressing for breakfast. The time at midmorning, when the kitchen had been a myriad of confused pots and pans and recipes, and the look in Bett's eyes when Billy had popped in the door with the three raccoons. Bett had dropped everything to fuss over them. If he hadn't slipped into the kitchen, that pot of sticky honey sauce would have boiled over on the stove. Then there'd been that special sexiness she radiated in the red dress . . . and his desire to maim when the so-called distinguished insurance salesman had picked up on it and dared to touch her.

He'd watched her. And his anger had kept growing. He'd accused her of letting Elizabeth undermine her confidence, her spirit, her values . . . their love. He'd been disappointed in her. Disappointed, angry, and . . .

Dead wrong.

He slipped off his shoes, turned off the lights downstairs, and mounted the stairs slowly in the darkness. Bett was no one's doormat. She never had been. She was an assertive, stubborn, strong-willed lady. The only time she turned into marshmallow was when there was a risk of hurting someone. She was terrible at hurting people—failed every time.

And for that, he'd turned on her? He was more than angry with himself; for days he'd been sick inside, not knowing how to make it right again, afraid anything he said would be wrong. Fear had built up in him, like a slow coiling spring, fear that he might have destroyed something that mattered more than life, that he might have hurt her in a way he could not make up for. The spring had coiled tight, too tight. His shoulders hadn't untensed in days; he'd barely slept; every muscle felt taut.

He stood for a moment before the closed door of their bedroom. He meant to push very quietly at the knob; instead, all his pent-up despair shoved at the door. It swung open, and Bett jerked around where she stood on the far side of the room by the window, her eyes huge and uncertain in her pale face. Her arms were wrapped around her chest, and the sudden vulnerable flush on her cheeks tore at his heart as she rushed toward him.

"Zach! I'm sorry. You are just going to have to listen to me, so don't start looking like that again. I've been wanting to tell you for days that I'm sorry—" Her hands fluttered up, her soft eyes brimming rapidly. "I couldn't wait for you to come home. Everything went wrong today. I know how it must have looked to you, that everything was for my mother, that I didn't care what you wanted. Zach, it wasn't intended that way. I wanted so much to show you—"

"Sh." The single syllable seemed to startle her. The coiled spring inside him seemed to uncoil at the speed of light. He was furious all over again that she was so unhappy. He took a step toward her, eyes blazing. And then, with a very gentle hand, pushed back a strand of hair on her cheek. "It wasn't *you*," he said earnestly. "*I* was wrong. Dammit, I never meant to hurt you. The thing with your mother was so important to you—I just wanted it to be right. For you, Bett. You were getting hurt, and I couldn't just stand there. But I shouldn't have pushed you."

"Of course you should have pushed. I was so wrapped up in it, I couldn't see. I *did* miss all the times we have together, all the feelings, all the simple conversations, and yet I kept letting it happen. It's all my fault—"

He surged forward, tugging her into his arms and wrapping her close, folding in the soft fabric of her dress, the scent of her, her silky hair. He wanted his touch to be soothing, and it wasn't. He couldn't hold her tightly enough. "Nothing," he growled, "was your fault. Nothing."

"It was."

"It wasn't."

"Zach—"

"Stop arguing with me." He tilted her head back with his thumbs on her chin. His lips came down on her trembling ones, his touch turning gentle. In his hold was all the fear of losing her. Nothing was as vulnerable as loving. Nothing felt as good as the feel of his wife close to him again.

"Zach." She stayed enfolded, but her eyes lifted to his, that frantic wariness gone but her face grave and still haunted with anxiety. "It was my fault, you know. I let the meaning of the two of us . . . slip away. I didn't see. So insensitive, Zach, but I honestly never believed that could happen. I never had to let my mother control—"

"Maybe," he agreed quietly. "I knew you could handle her, Bett. And I knew if you finally did, you'd be happier." His fingers brushed back her hair. "I also happen to love you, you know. I love your softness and your giving. And to expect you suddenly to turn hard as nails was stupid on my part. Stupid and wrong."

"It wasn't wrong." She leaned her cheek into his palm. "I never meant to—"

"Are you *still* arguing?" His tone was half humorous, half genuinely exasperated. And *all* loving.

Her eyes searched his face. The love she saw there was a fierce thing, even while he was trying to coax her into a smile. "You had a right to be angry," she said quietly. "And... hurt. I know I hurt you. I..."

"No," he murmured. "I hurt you." His hands slid around her back, his mouth dipping down to the curve of her shoulder. So damn stupid, to be angry she wasn't tougher inside, tough and hardhearted. Tough and strong were not the same thing at all. Every year they'd been married, she'd grown in confidence; he'd swelled with love, watching her. He wanted her to grow—not toughen, just grow. But it was long past time for him to make love to the lady she was, to make very sure she understood that he loved her just as she was. His palms slid down, cupping her slim hips. His lips found a delectable spot in the curve of her shoulder.

She yielded like Eve, with a sigh that seemed to flow through her body. She wrapped her arms around him and just held on, still trembling, her face buried in his shoulder. And for once, the knock on the door didn't make her stiffen suddenly into a statue. Zach pressed his lips firmly on hers, drawing back. "I'll handle it," he said quietly.

"*No*. I will." Bett pulled away from him. Elizabeth *was* her mother. This was exactly the time to prove it. All day she'd been trying to show him that she had her priorities back in order. When she pulled open the door, her eyes were brilliant, fired with determination.

Elizabeth, on the other side of the doorway, looked delectably vulnerable in her pink ruffled robe. "I was hoping you were awake, Brittany. There's something I've been trying to tell you all day—"

"Mom, I'm exhausted. So is Zach."

"I never told you about Harold Baker. You know, the

man who owns the bookstore in Silver Oaks? And it's been bothering me that I haven't told you. Brittany, we've been meeting for lunch. And . . . more than lunch. Actually—"

Bett didn't hear a thing. "I promise, Mom, we'll talk in the morning. For just as long as you want, but right now—"

"I've been seeing him. And he . . . asked me to marry him."

"I absolutely love you to bits, Mom," Bett said blindly. "I know you can't sleep; I wish I could help you with that. I *will* help you; maybe we can get an appointment for you with a doctor tomorrow. But right now, you're just going to have to forgive me—I'm exhausted. Okay?"

Elizabeth sighed. "Of course. I—good night, darling."

Bett closed the door, and whirled back to Zach. His arms felt like coming home. Zach held her close, and with a crooked smile, felt her cuddling, surrendering form turn stiff as her mother's words sank in. *"No,"* she murmured into his shoulder.

"Open the door, two bits."

"No."

"It's all right," he whispered into her hair. "This is different."

"She had to have made that up."

"Open the door."

"All day. *All day* I have been trying to show you how very much more you matter to me than my mother. Or than turkeys and holidays. Or than other people. Every single thing that could possibly go wrong with this day went wrong—"

His lips brushed her forehead. "Open the door."

Five minutes later, the three of them were having instant coffee in the kitchen. "Now, he isn't particularly good-looking," Elizabeth said nervously. "But he plays canasta. So do I. He stays up until all hours of the night, can't sleep. And he talks, all the time. I just...every time I've been in town I've found myself going there. We have coffee in the back and he takes me out to lunch. And three of the dinners—I didn't tell you, Brittany. You were all for my going out, but this was...different. I knew it was different. And I thought you would feel I was being disloyal to your father—"

"Mom, that isn't so," Bett rushed in compassionately. "But for heaven's sake, you can't have known him very long."

"Well, these three months. We're hardly planning on a shotgun wedding, but at our age, there isn't much point in our waiting, either. The thing is—you two. Whether you'd object—"

Zach and Bett exchanged a fleeting glance. "We don't object," Zach said quietly. "As long as you're happy."

"He's such a fool. He just *won't* take care of himself if he doesn't have a woman around," Elizabeth said distractedly. "He likes being bossed, he tells me. Not that I'm the bossy type—"

Bett's lips parted. Zach laid a repressive hand on her knee. "You certainly aren't," he agreed.

"I don't want either of you to think I've done anything...immoral—"

Bett debated for a second and a half whether to advise her mother that, truthfully, she'd better kick around an immoral action or two before she made any permanent commitments. Zach's hand anchored on her knee again. "We never thought that," he assured his mother-in-law.

"I never would," Elizabeth said.

"I'm sure of that."

Zach had the sneaking suspicion that the lady had compromised her...morals. Bett *had* to get her genes from somewhere. Chet undoubtedly contributed the dominant portion, but someone had to have been on the receiving end.

"And I came here to help you," Elizabeth said worriedly. "It's not that I want to desert you now."

"Mom, you wouldn't be," Bett said swiftly. Elizabeth didn't appear to notice any frantically enthusiastic notes.

It was one in the morning before the three of them trudged back upstairs. Zach, once the bedroom door had closed, reached for Bett, hauled her up into his arms, and laid her giggling form on their bed. Seconds later, he collapsed next to her.

"Some matchmaker you are," he scolded. "She ended up having to do all the work herself." His words came out in whispers, in breaths that fanned the tender skin of her throat. He turned her until her stomach was against the mattress, making it easy for him to unzip the back of her dress. It was a long zipper, ending at the base of her spine. And it was going to take him a very long time to get it down, if he was going to kiss her exposed skin lingeringly at inch intervals.

"You didn't do any better than I did," Bett whispered back, her voice muffled in the comforter.

"Do you even know Harold?"

"Are you joking? In the winter, I live in that bookstore. I've known him ever since we moved here."

"So?"

"So, he's perfect. So why didn't *you* invite him to the house?"

Her favorite red dress was suddenly pulled over her head and landed on the floor beside the bed. She peered over the side of the mattress, staring at it. Zach was kissing her vertebrae, one by one. Given an ounce of encouragement, he wouldn't last for a minute and a half. But then, given an ounce of weakness, she was afraid she wouldn't last either. But how long could a person stare at one wrinkling red dress?

"Why didn't *I?* How about, why didn't *you* ask him?" He'd forgotten the exact look of Bett's back, from spine to bottom to calves. He was usually obsessed with the front of her. He skimmed off her panty hose, a task he'd mastered over the years, this time made slightly easier by the fact that her legs were dangling over the side of the bed. The curve of her spine ended in a delightful raise of fanny; Bett had beautiful thighs.

"It was your project. Getting my mother married off." She rolled to her back, regarding Zach in the semidarkness. He certainly seemed to be in a terrible hurry to remove his clothes.

"It appears she *is* married off," he said flatly. His naked weight made a serious depression in the mattress.

"Yes." Her hands reached for him. Her fingers gently touched his firm cheekbones, then slid into his hair. "Yes," she echoed vaguely.

"That was never the point, you know," he whispered. He slid up, his bare skin against her bare skin. His fingertips, too, found her cheekbones, then her hair. "Not marrying her off, two bits. Just you and me. Lost and found. I don't think we'll play tag with losing each other again. It wasn't much fun."

"No," she agreed.

Without warning, his voice turned quiet. "I was there, Bett," Zach said roughly. "We were never really lost."

When he pulled her to him so very tightly, she held on. But that wasn't entirely true, she thought. One could lose love, and she'd needed to learn that. It was precious knowledge, because they would have a child in time, and their priorities probably would get confused again . . . but never quite so confused. Love was so precious that one could never take it for granted. Love was that vulnerable. That strong. That worth holding on to.

WONDERFUL ROMANCE NEWS:

Do you know about the exciting SECOND CHANCE AT LOVE/TO HAVE AND TO HOLD newsletter? Are you on our *free* mailing list? If reading all about your favorite authors, getting sneak previews of their latest releases, and being filled in on all the latest happenings and events in the romance world sound good to you, then you'll love our SECOND CHANCE AT LOVE and TO HAVE AND TO HOLD Romance News.

If you'd like to be added to our mailing list, just fill out the coupon below and send it in...and we'll send you your *free* newsletter every three months — hot off the press.

☐ *Yes, I would like to receive your free SECOND CHANCE AT LOVE/TO HAVE AND TO HOLD newsletter.*

Name _____

Address _____

City _____ **State/Zip** _____

Please return this coupon to:

Berkley Publishing
200 Madison Avenue, New York, New York 10016
Att: Rebecca Kaufman

HERE'S WHAT READERS ARE SAYING ABOUT

To Have and to Hold

"Your TO HAVE AND TO HOLD series is a fabulous and long overdue idea."
— *A. D., Upper Darby, PA**

"I have been reading romance novels for over ten years and feel the TO HAVE AND TO HOLD series is the best I have read. It's exciting, sensitive, refreshing, well written. Many thanks for a series of books I can relate to."
— *O. K., Bensalem, PA**

"I enjoy your books tremendously."
— *J. C., Houston, TX**

"I love the books and read them over and over."
— *E. K., Warren, MI**

"You have another winner with the new TO HAVE AND TO HOLD series."
— *R. P., Lincoln Park, MI**

"I love the new series TO HAVE AND TO HOLD."
— *M. L., Cleveland, OH**

"I've never written a fan letter before, but TO HAVE AND TO HOLD is fantastic."
— *E. S., Narberth, PA**

*Name and address available upon request